Three Summers

also by Judith Clarke

Angels Passing By
Night Train
The Lost Day
The Heroic Life of Al Capsella
Al Capsella and the Watchdogs
Al Capsella on Holidays
Friend of My Heart
The Boy on the Lake
Panic Stations
The Ruin of Kevin O'Reilly
Luna Park at Night
Big Night Out
Wolf on the Fold
Starry Nights
Kalpana's Dream
One Whole and Perfect Day
The Winds of Heaven

JUDITH CLARKE was born in Sydney and educated at the University of New South Wales and the Australian National University in Canberra. She has worked as a teacher and librarian, and in adult education in Victoria and New South Wales.

Judith's novels include the multi-award-winning *Wolf on the Fold*, as well as *Friend of my Heart*, *Night Train*, and the very popular and funny *Al Capsella* series. *Kalpana's Dream* was an Honor Book in the 2005 Boston Globe-Horn Book Awards; *One Whole and Perfect Day* was a winner in the 2007 Queensland Premier's Literary Awards, shortlisted in the 2007 CBCA Book of the Year Awards and the NSW Premier's Literary Awards, and Honor Book in the American Library Association, Michael L. Printz Awards for Excellence in Young Adult Literature 2008. *The Winds of Heaven* was shortlisted for the 2010 Prime Minister's Literary Awards, Young Adult Fiction, and the 2010 CBCA Book of the Year Awards.

Judith's books have been published in the USA and Europe to high acclaim.

Three Summers

JUDITH CLARKE

ALLEN&UNWIN
SYDNEY · MELBOURNE · AUCKLAND · LONDON

First published in 2012

Copyright © Judith Clarke 2012

Allen & Unwin
83 Alexander Street
Crows Nest NSW 2065
Australia
Phone: (61 2) 8425 0100
Fax: (61 2) 9906 2218
Email: info@allenandunwin.com
Web: www.allenandunwin.com

A Cataloguing-in-Publication entry is available from the
National Library of Australia
www.trove.nla.gov.au

ISBN 978 1 74237 827 5

Cover and text design by Ruth Grüner
Cover photos by Rebecca Parker/Trevillion Images and iStockphoto
Set in 10.5 pt Sabon by Ruth Grüner
Printed and bound in Australia by Griffin Press

1 3 5 7 9 10 8 6 4 2

The paper in this book is FSC® certified.
FSC® promotes environmentally responsible,
socially beneficial and economically viable
management of the world's forests.

To dear Frances Floyd

PART ONE

Secret Places

one

Ruth woke from a dream of Tam Finn, so vivid that for a moment its landscape – the narrow stretch of coarse sand beside the creek, the ripple of brown water over the pebbles, the broad shiny leaves of the bushes on the far bank – seemed more real than the familiar furniture of her room. She sat up, throwing the covers back, breathing hard, while the brown water and the shiny bushes flickered and faded, sucked into a mist which thinned and then vanished, leaving nothing behind except a suspicion that ordinary things were not as solid as they appeared.

She leaned back against the pillows and thought about Tam Finn. Why had she dreamed about him? She hardly knew him; he was the boy from *Fortuna*, the big property five miles down the Old Western Highway where her nan had worked when she was a girl. He'd been in Ruth's class the year before last, but only for a little while. She saw him in town occasionally, and heard the gossip that went round, that was all. And yet in the dream he'd been sitting close beside her on the sand, leaning into her; even awake she could still feel the weight of his body pressed against her side, his arm tight around her, his strong fingers digging into the flesh above her elbow. Such closeness should have felt strange yet instead it seemed oddly familiar. It was like those times when she saw him in town; how the mere glimpse of his pale face beneath the tumble of blue-black curls would bring such a deep shiver of recognition that for a moment she'd feel she could walk right up to him and say, 'Here I am,' and Tam Finn would smile at her as if they were old friends.

She sighed and closed her eyes, drifting back into the dream, feeling the weight of his body again, the fingers digging into her arm, a flutter of warm breath against her cheek. A girl's voice said clearly, 'But what if you don't know who you are?' and Ruth struggled awake again, suddenly afraid. She knew the voice; it belonged to Helen Hogan. Not Helen as she was now, seventeen, grown up, but Helen when they were little kids in the playground, telling stories to each other in the shade of the peppercorn trees.

You could walk out of your house in your sleep, Helen had told them, right into the street where you could meet anyone. It might be a perfect stranger, someone you'd never seen before, or it could be a person you knew and really hated, but none of this would matter, you'd still – here Helen had lowered her voice and whispered, 'do it with him.' When she'd said this, the listening girls had looked at each other and giggled. Ellie Lester had crossed her eyes. They'd been in grade four, nine years old, but they'd known all sorts of things.

It was strange, thought Ruth, how she could remember that whole long-ago conversation: all the words and even the little gasps and silences, how Fee had been wearing a yellow sundress and Helen's plaits had been tied with two big bows of red tartan ribbon. She could even remember the weather: hot, really hot, full summer, the shade of the peppercorn trees no more than a faint grey dappling on the dry ground.

'Yes!' Helen had gone on. 'You can do it with *anyone* in your sleep, and not even know! And if another person comes along and wakes you while you're doing it, well—' here Helen had drawn in a long breath and finished dramatically, 'well, then you die!'

Kathy Ryan had gasped, 'Oh!' and put her hand across her mouth.

'It's true!' Helen had insisted, tossing her long heavy plaits back over her shoulders and staring at the other girls defiantly. The plaits were blue-black and shiny, glossy as a crow's wing.

None of them had believed the story, at least not in the daytime.

'That's bullshit!' Fee Lachlan had protested. 'It's bullshit, Helen!'

'Yeah?'

'Yeah. My mum says that when you sleepwalk, you can't do anything you wouldn't do if you were awake. She says you can't do anything that isn't really *you*.'

That was when Helen said the thing that had somehow found its way into Ruth's dream. *'But what if you don't know who you really are?'* The words had come out very clear and separate, like footsteps down an empty hall, and there'd been a funny little silence beneath the peppercorn trees. It was as if those words had been important in a way they couldn't quite understand. Important, and scary too.

5

It's why they'd come back to her now, thought Ruth, after years and years.

Her arm was burning. She switched on the bedside lamp and carefully examined the tender skin above her elbow, half expecting to find the red marks of Tam Finn's fingertips there.

The arm was unmarked. There was nothing. Ruth clicked her tongue in the way her nan did when she was knitting and dropped a stitch. Of course there was no mark; you didn't get marks from a dream, however real it seemed, just like you didn't make love in a dream and have it turn out to be real. '*But what if you don't know who you really are?*' Helen's voice echoed faintly, but this time Ruth took no notice; she was properly awake now, and she could tell by the brightness of the light at the edges of the blind that it was late, well after nine. She could hear her dad moving round in the shop downstairs, the sound of a heavy sack being dragged across the floor, the clang of the metal lid on the big flour bin and then the squeak of the screen door and a voice calling, 'Morning, Mr Gower,' and Dad's gentle voice replying, 'Morning Mrs Harrison, what can I do for you this lovely day?'

She switched off the lamp. The bedrooms above the shop were silent; Nan would be out in her garden by now. She always got up early. 'It was a habit I learned at the orphanage,' she'd told Ruth once.

'And never got out of,' Ruth said.

'Never,' Nan had replied. She'd been smiling. But there were other times, like certain dark winter afternoons when Nan would stand at the window gazing out at the rain, when Ruth could see the orphanage in her eyes, like a shadow, and then she felt she'd do anything to keep that shadow away.

She loved her nan.

'Don't you mind not having a mum?' her best friend Fee had asked on their very first day at school.

Ruth had thought about it for a moment. 'Yes,' she'd said at last. 'But I've got my nan.'

Fee had taken Ruth's hand and looked gravely into her new friend's face. 'And me,' she'd said. 'You've got me now.'

TWELVE years on, they were still best friends. 'Tam Finn's back,' Fee had told her yesterday morning, and Ruth's heart had jumped. She hadn't thought of Tam Finn for ages, and yet the moment Fee had spoken his name her heart had given that strange little leap, as if it had a secret life of its own and knew things that Ruth didn't know.

'Back?' she'd echoed stupidly.

'Got kicked out of Ag School, didn't he?'

It was no surprise. Tam Finn had been kicked out of two private colleges; that was the reason he'd been at their school for those brief few months. The teachers hadn't liked him.

'How do you know he got kicked out of Ag School?'

'Joanie Fawkes at the post office, who else?' Fee answered. 'She told Mum Mr Finn and Tam had this big fight in the middle of Main Street and Mr Finn was roaring out how he was going to leave *Fortuna* to someone else if Tam didn't change his ways.'

'What ways?'

'Girls, I s'pose, you know what Tam Finn's like – people

say that's why he got kicked out of those other schools. Joanie Fawkes does, anyway.'

'Joanie Fawkes is a stupid old gossip!' Ruth had cried, and Fee had glanced at her curiously, surprised at the anger in her friend's voice. 'And she steams the letters open, I bet,' Ruth added more calmly.

'Course she does. All the same, it's best to know things sometimes.' Fee had given Ruth a funny, sidelong glance. 'Pity Helen Hogan doesn't.'

'Helen Hogan?'

'She's been going with him. This mate of Mattie's saw them down the creek – you know, down the little beach, mucking round. Her dad's going to kill her if he finds out; he'll have the hide off her, for sure.'

Ruth flinched, thinking of Helen Hogan's skin, her *hide*, which was a pure and perfect white with faint blue shadows, like new milk.

That was why she'd remembered the scene in the playground, of course – because Fee had been talking about Helen yesterday, and she'd had the dream about Tam Finn because Fee had been talking about him as well.

Though there was something else. Yesterday afternoon the house had been so hot that she had taken a book and gone down to the creek to read. The brown water had trickled over the stones, crickets chirped, birds called drowsily in the trees – and then there'd been another sound, a rustling in the bushes on the other bank, and something that could have been a long, long sigh. Looking up, she thought she'd seen a narrow wedge of pale face framed in those broad green leaves: a pale face, curly black hair, grey eyes staring straight across at her.

She'd jumped to her feet and scrambled up the bank towards the road. No one had followed. The road was as empty as the afternoon.

She'd imagined it, of course she had. It hadn't been Tam Finn amongst those bushes, only light and shadow and strange little games going on your mind that someone else seemed to be playing, perhaps that person Helen Hogan said you didn't know you were. Tam Finn wouldn't be spying on her down at the creek; she wasn't his type. 'Anyone's his type,' Fee would say. 'Anyone.'

'Not me,' said Ruth aloud, and she slid out of bed and went to stand in front of the wardrobe mirror. 'Not *you*,' she told the girl in the old blue nightie with her hair all tangled and messy from sleep. '*You're* not his type at all, whatever these funny feelings. Fun-ny feel-ings,' she chanted, rising up on her toes and then down again, smiling at the serious face of the girl in the mirror, making her smile back, a little uncertainly. 'And anyway,' she added, '*you're* going away soon, you're going to Sydney University.'

Two

Only she mightn't be. Living in Sydney, going to the university – Ruth's new life, as her nan kept on calling it – was hanging in the air, suspended like some shining miraculous treasure, just out of reach. Everything depended on how well she'd done in the exams.

'You *love* exams!' Fee had accused her gleefully when time was up and pens put down and the two of them burst out from the very last afternoon of school.

'Who, me?'

'Yes, *you*.' Fee had flung her old school case down and given it a kick along the ground.

'How do you know?'

'Finished early, didn't I? And then we weren't allowed to go outside and there was nothing to do so I was watching you. *Your face!* You looked like – a kind of happy angel.'

'An angel!'

'Honestly! Anyone could tell from that face you're going to come top of the state.'

'Angels don't come top of the state. Or people from Barinjii.'

'Always a first time. You will, I bet! And then – then you'll go flying far, far away.'

'You're as bad as Nan!'

Fee's slender arms had flown out in a wide clear gesture. 'You'll fly away over the great wide world, and never come back, and I'll never ever see you again.'

Ruth had laughed; it was impossible to think that she'd never see Fee again. Fee was for always.

'Course you'll see me. I'd come back, even if I did go away; can't miss your wedding, can I? Specially since I'm going to be bridesmaid and wear that awful purple shroud.'

'It's not purple; it's lilac! And it's not a shroud!'

'Anyway, I mightn't even be going; it depends on the results.'

'If it depends on them, you're on your way. And I can *feel* you're going; best friends always know.'

Fee was staying in Barinjii. Love made her world go round: she loved Barinjii and she loved Mattie Howe and they were getting married at Easter. 'I'm going to stay here and be a mum,' she'd said, nudging the battered school case further along the road. 'Keep the home flag flying, eh?'

It was a kind of joke, but Ruth knew Fee was truly happy; she could see it in her shining eyes and the way her feet had skipped in a little dance on the dusty road. 'Oh, last exam!' she'd exclaimed joyfully. 'My last exam forever! Oh, I'm so glad – glad, glad, glad! It was torture sitting at that desk for hours. It was torture being at school. All those years! And now I'm free!' She'd given the old case one last kick and sent it sliding into the long grass of the verge. 'Free, free, free!'

AS for Nan, there'd been no stopping her. 'You'll be needing new things,' she'd announced over breakfast the very first day after the exams.

'New things?'

'Clothes!' Her small face had been almost swallowed by her smile. 'For when you start at university!'

'But Nan, it's too soon! What if I don't get enough marks?'

'Of course you'll get enough marks. More than enough. Your teachers tell me you're a certainty.'

'But—'

It was no use. The very next day they'd gone into Dubbo on the bus, to the biggest department store in town and bought the material: linen and cotton for summer, wool and cord for winter, zips and buttons and sewing thread and braid. Nan had sewed for days, the needle of her old Singer flashing down the long seams of straight skirts and flared skirts, gathering fullness into narrow waistbands, tracking carefully round the curves of collars and the armholes of dresses and blouses. In the evenings they'd turned up hems and sewed on buttons and zips and braid, while Dad sat reading the paper in his armchair, and from the mantelpiece above his head Ruth's mother Polly, who'd died when Ruth was a baby, smiled down at them from her silver frame. Ruth had no real memory of Polly, though sometimes at night she'd have an occasional fleeting sense, right on the border of sleep, of being rocked and held, of great delighted eyes gazing into hers, and a gentle hand cupping her head, leaving its warmth behind.

'Your mother would be so *proud* of you,' Nan had said last night, and Ruth had needed to bite hard on her bottom lip to stop herself from crying out again, 'But Nan, it's too *soon*.'

Now she swung open the door of her wardrobe and reached inside. She took out the brown linen skirt with the saddle-stitched side pockets and ivory buttons from the waist to the hem. 'For best,' Nan had said, 'for when you get asked to some special occasion in Sydney.'

'Some special occasion!' Ruth had scoffed, because that was Nan all over, imagining special occasions and unknown people who would ask her to them, imagining a whole *life* for her, before anything was certain, making plans with such excitement you'd think that imaginary life was hers.

Ruth stared at the skirt for a long moment, struggling to imagine that far-off special evening, the unknown room where she would dress up in this skirt and her new best blouse, stand in front of a different mirror to brush her hair, getting ready to go out. The picture wouldn't come; she had never liked parties; Nan's 'special occasion' didn't seem like her. She touched the top button of the skirt and her hand jumped back as if the cold ivory had given off a small electric shock. But it was an image from the dream of Tam Finn that had shocked her, rushing in suddenly from that other world: how Tam Finn had laid a fingertip right in the very centre of her forehead, and it had felt exactly like this button, cold as old, old bone.

She slid the skirt back onto the rail and closed the wardrobe. Down in the street, the dogs began to bark, first the high shrill yap of Fancy, old Mrs Tregoar's little Pomeranian at number 81, then the deep roar of Kray, Mal Burton's big

Alsatian at number 89. 'Shut up, you silly bugger,' Mal was bellowing.

Ruth's heart seemed to freeze beneath the thin stuff of her nightie, as it did every morning when the postman came. Up at the school the teachers had told them the exam results would come either this week or the next. Today was Friday, and Ruth had given up on this week, because letters hardly ever seemed to come on Friday. Next week then, she'd told herself yesterday when Fred Fawkes had sailed right by their door. Monday, perhaps. Things took a long time to reach Barinjii and when they arrived they smelled of the Western Express, of diesel oil and tobacco smoke, of dry curled sandwiches and boredom and heat and dust.

She crossed to the window and pulled up the blind. Fred Fawkes was cycling slowly down the footpath on their side of the street. She watched him slide two letters into Dr Tierney's box at number 103 and then ride on past the Carver place, half vanishing in the shadows of the big trees that lined the vacant lot next door. A moment later he came into sight at the very edge of their shop and rode on so close beneath her window she could see the comb marks running in greasy ridges through his brylcreemed hair. *Clack!* went their letter flap and panic squeezed at her heart again, because what if it was *the* letter? And what if her marks weren't good enough after all? Not even for the teachers' college out at Dubbo?

'The teachers' college!' Nan would sniff whenever Ruth mentioned it. 'We can do better than that!' How would Nan feel if Ruth couldn't even get in there, if she had to stay in Barinjii and wear her nan's beautiful new clothes to serve in the shop? Or to work in the bank or the Shire Council office, waiting for some boy to come along so she could get engaged like all the other girls? And that boy wouldn't be Tam Finn, because even if she *had* been his type, everyone knew that Tam Finn wasn't the marrying kind. The men from *Fortuna* married late, and when they did marry, it wasn't to a Barinjii girl: the Finns married girls of their own sort, girls from the great properties further west, girls who'd never been behind a counter or made their own clothes or even stood trembling at a window, waiting for the postman to bring a letter which could change their lives.

And that letter was lying down there in the hall; she could *feel* it. She ran from her room and stood at the top of the stairs, peering down over the banister, along the dark passage to the door, where a single long white envelope was lying face down on the carpet beneath the letter slot. It could be anything: an electricity bill or a rates notice or a letter from one of the shop's suppliers, but her heart hammered wildly as she went on down the stairs because she *knew*, and when she reached the door she stood there for a moment, quite still, before stretching out one bare foot and turning the letter over.

Miss Ruth Gower,
109 Main Street,
Barinjii, NSW

It was the one. A thick white envelope with a crest in its corner. *The* crest; the one she'd first seen on the application forms Miss Austin had helped her to fill in at school: the broad-armed cross with an open book lying in its centre, the curly maned lion prancing above it, one paw raised jauntily. '*Sidere mens eadum mutato*,' Miss Austin had read out, and then translated, '*Though the constellation is changed, the mind is universal.*' She'd looked up at Ruth with her small bright twinkling eyes. 'They were thinking of the great English universities when they decided on that motto, Ruth, places like Oxford and Cambridge' – her voice had lingered on the famous names – 'all under the northern sky, my dear. And they wanted to say that though their new university at Sydney was under a different sky, its pursuit of excellence would be the same.'

They'd been standing at the window of the tiny shack-like library of Barinjii High, which was nothing more than a single smallish room, with shelves on three sides and one long table in the centre with a dozen chairs arranged around it. A blotchy view of Barinjii painted by the headmaster's wife hung above the shelf of reference books; Mrs Elton had got the wheat silo on a lean, it looked as if it was about to tumble gently into Ed Howe's timber yard. Outside the window lay a field of trampled grass where a late-winter wind was tossing dust and bits of chaff, beyond the field was an unsealed road and then miles and miles of straw-coloured paddocks beneath a high blue sky. Miss Austin had stared out across the paddocks, repeating dreamily, 'the pursuit of excellence.' Then she'd sighed and said, 'That's what life should be about, always!' and her bright eyes had scanned Ruth's face again. 'Remember that, my dear. Remember it. Whatever sky's above you.'

Ruth snatched up the envelope and held it close against her chest. 'Please, oh please,' she whispered, and then slid a fingernail beneath the flap, and drew out the two thick sheets inside. *Dear Miss Gower,* she read, *we are pleased to inform you that*— 'Oh thank you! Thank you!' breathed Ruth, because it was all right, it must be all right because if they were pleased it surely meant she'd got the scholarship – her eyes raced on down the page and there were the longed-for words at last: 'full scholarship' and 'living allowance' and then her marks on the second page, four As and two First Class Honours, in English and History. She'd be going to Sydney!

And Nan wouldn't be disappointed, she wouldn't get that bleak orphanage expression in her eyes. Ruth brushed the sheets against her lips, she kissed them. 'Thank you! Thank you! Thank you!' she cried again, and then went perfectly still, wanting to fix the moment in her memory forever: this Friday morning in January, 1959, standing in the shabby hallway in her old blue nightie, the crested letter clutched fast, the shaft of yellow light spilled across the faded carpet from the kitchen's open door.

And Tam Finn was gone. The boy from *Fortuna* dropped from her mind like a stone down a well, sinking beneath the deep dark water without a sound. She'd made it all up, those strange feelings about him, that sense of recognition and familiarity, it had been dreams, the stuff of long dull summer holidays – how else could it so suddenly drop away?

'Nan!' she called, rushing down the hall and through the kitchen to the back door, the letter held fast, the letter which would make everything new. She flung the door open, the light burst on her, the green of the garden, the great blue sky above. 'Nan!' she cried, waving the letter, waving it wildly, 'Nan! *Nan!* Look! It's come!'

three

When she'd come out into the garden this morning, Ruth's nan had been seized by a wonderful idea. It was the hydrangeas – the wonderful shining blueness of them the moment she'd opened the back door, the great blooms seeming to float in the air, their rounded shapes like the billows of a picture-book sea. She'd take a big basket of them up to Saint Columba's; she'd arrange them round the feet of the little Virgin; it would make her look like a young girl stepping out into a sunlit sea.

Father Joseph had rescued the small wooden statue from an abandoned church out Carpina way. 'They'd left her there!' he'd exclaimed indignantly to Margaret May. 'Can you imagine that, Maidie? The sheer bloody heartlessness of it! Leaving her stuck out there in all weathers, standing in the heat and wind and rain!'

Left her there. The phrase had trembled in the air between them and Margaret May had remembered early mornings in the orphanage, waking up while the others were still asleep and feeling exactly like that: how she'd been left there. 'Oh yes,' she'd said softly, 'I can imagine it.'

Father Joseph had stared at her. 'You can?'

'Heartlessness,' she'd said. 'I can imagine that.'

'Ah, Maidie,' he'd sighed. He was an old fool sometimes but she had a kind of tenderness for him; his was one of the first faces she'd seen on earth. It was Father Joseph who'd brought her to the nuns, from the hospital – where a young girl had been forced to give her child away – and sometimes Margaret May thought she had a memory of that night, of the sulky rattling through dark country, of lying inside it looking up at a field of bright stars. There'd been a smell of tobacco and horse.

She cut the big blooms carefully, picturing the way they'd look when she'd arranged them in the church, with the light shining down from the big window. She hummed as she worked, because these days there was a special happiness inside her at the thought of her Ruthie's new life down in Sydney; away from the confines of Barinjii, she knew her granddaughter's life would open like a flower. Her own life had been like a series of prisons: first the orphanage, then the skivvying at *Fortuna*, then Don – but none of that mattered now because Ruth would get away.

When the basket was full, she picked a bunch of fresh basil from the herb bed and tucked it in beside the flowers. The ground in this sunny spot was dry and she filled the big green watering can and brought it back along the sandy path. Two big magpies hovered round her feet with glistening eyes, watching the water trickle down from the nozzle of the can. She took up a trowel, scooped a small depression in the earth and filled it with water. 'There you are,' she told them.

'Quickly now, before it soaks away,' and the big birds stepped forward delicately and bent their glossy heads to drink.

Dragging the heavy can along the path had made her feel a little breathless and she sat down on the bench for a moment, one hand pressed to her heart, gazing up at the translucent sky. On mornings like this she could feel a kind of glory over the earth, a tender veil thrown down from heaven: the small breeze fluttering the leaves, the scents of thyme and lavender and basil trembling in the air, the climbing roses in full bloom, a great fall of pink and white tumbling down the warm stone wall.

Father Joseph had built that wall for her only a few weeks after her husband Don had drowned. He'd brought the stones from the old quarry in the battered ute he'd had in those days, taking her two older boys with him for the ride. He'd laid the stones slowly, carefully, while Charlie and Vin skittered round his feet, and Margaret May had sat on this very bench nursing the baby, Ray. Father Joseph had worked in silence, never saying a word about the dead man or God's mercy or Don finding peace at last – he'd known she couldn't bear to hear any of that, he'd known she'd hated Don.

'Nan!'

The magpies flew up in a rush. Ruth was tearing down the path towards her, still in her old blue nightie, barefoot, hair all tangled, waving a long white envelope, and when she saw that envelope Margaret May's old heart jumped. She stood up.

'Nan! It's come!'

Margaret May held out her hand and took the letter gently, almost reverently. She saw the crest on the envelope, and Ruth's shining, happy eyes, and her own eyes lit even before she'd slipped the two sheets from the envelope and read them quickly through. 'Oh Ruthie!' she gasped, flinging her arms round the girl's slight body, holding her tight, and then stepping back to survey her granddaughter lovingly, every inch of her, from the crown of her head to the long toes of her bare brown dusty feet. 'I knew you'd get it,' she breathed. 'I knew, I *knew*.'

'M'mm.' Ruth stretched her long arms up into the shining air. 'I didn't.'

'You didn't?'

'I was worried, Nan,' the girl confided in a rush. 'I thought I might only have *imagined* I'd done well. I thought I might only get enough marks to go to teachers' college—'

'Teachers' college!'

Now that the letter had come Ruth could laugh at the disgusted expression on Nan's face. 'Or not even *there*!' she cried. 'I thought I might have to get a job at a bank, or stay home and help Dad in the shop.'

Margaret May drew in a quick, sharp breath. 'Ah no,' she said. 'Not you.'

'It *could* have been me, Nan.' There was something in her nan's refusal to doubt her that Ruth found worrying, even disturbing. It was like a hand pressed against her chest, squeezing out the breath. She stared into her grandmother's flushed face with a little frown. 'I was afraid of letting you down,' she said, and it was true, for in these long weeks of waiting the thought of Nan's disappointment had kept waking her up in the night.

Margaret May shook her head. 'Letting me down, that's not important. It's letting yourself down that counts.'

'But sometimes I think—'

Margaret May was quick. 'What do you think?'

'Oh, nothing.'

'Something, or you would have said.'

'It's—' Ruth bit her lip and frowned. 'Sometimes I think I don't know what I want, not really.' Because it had come over her, the second she ran through the kitchen door and the loveliness of the garden had burst on her like a wave, its colours and scents, its markings of sunlight and shade, the bees humming and Nan sitting there on the bench, her face turning towards her – how soon all of this would be far away, and she didn't want it to be. It was almost like she wanted to stay. And yet she wanted to go, too. I hardly know who I *am*, she thought, and at once heard Helen Hogan's nine-year-old voice saying, 'But what if you don't know who you really are?'

'It's like I'm half asleep sometimes, Nan,' she confided. 'In a sort of dream.' She rubbed at her eyes, confused, and suddenly Tam Finn was back again, swinging across her mind like some cold, enormous bell. An image of his white face in a thicket of green leaves struck her so sharply that she hardly heard Nan saying, 'You'll wake up in Sydney.'

'What?'

Nan smiled and repeated, 'You'll wake up in Sydney. You'll love it there.'

'M'mm.' Ruth could still see Tam Finn's face. His grey eyes were the colour of rain. 'Oh, I don't know,' she sighed.

Nan sat down on the bench. She reached out her hand and

pulled Ruth gently down beside her. 'Ruthie, now listen,' she said, 'This place is your home and I know you love it, but here every day is the same, more or less. In Sydney, every day will bring something new!'

'I like every day being the same.'

'You think you do, *now*, but later on you might hate it, Ruthie.' Margaret May's voice took on a sudden vehemence, it was as if there was a fire burning down inside her, ready to burst out. 'Waking up every morning to the same old round, day after day after day, that's one way to live, certainly, but for some people it's not enough, Ruthie.'

'I suppose so,' said Ruth doubtfully, and a scarce second later, without even meaning to, she cried out, 'But Nan, it's so *far*!'

Margaret May's face became stern, a fierce light gleamed in her eyes. 'Far doesn't matter,' she said, looking down at the letter in her hands. She stroked the crest, running her finger along the lion's curly mane. 'You're going to have such a wonderful time at the university. You'll meet all kinds of people, people you can talk to about the things that matter—'

'I can talk to Fee. We talk about things that matter.'

'Of course you do. But there are other things, so many other things, Ruthie—' Margaret May spread her hands. 'A girl like you should see the world.'

'You didn't,' countered Ruth.

'That was different. Those were harder times.' Margaret May looked out into the distance and the orphanage shadow came into her eyes. Ruth could hardly bear to think of the place where Nan had grown up, abandoned now, though you could still see it from the highway, all turrets and towers and barred windows on top of its rock-strewn hill.

'See those rocks up there?' Nan had said one afternoon when they were passing in the bus. 'They were one of the punishments.'

'How do you mean?'

'We had to pick those rocks up and cart them around to the back on Saturday afternoons. Big as babies some of them were, and didn't they tear up our hands! And you know, however many we moved, there still seemed just as many next time. We said the nuns made the big girls carry them back to the front at night when we little ones were asleep.'

'What did they punish you for?'

'Just for being there. Because we were the children of sin.'

'But it wasn't *your* sin.'

'It wasn't anyone's.'

After the orphanage her grandmother had been been sent to *Fortuna* to work as a housemaid. 'Nan, what was it like at *Fortuna*?' Ruth asked now. Her voice lingered on the beautiful name; she had a longing to hear the great house described because it was Tam Finn's house, the place where his family had lived for generations. She felt she would give a little piece of her heart to see its rooms and passages, the famous garden with its lawns and flower beds and peacock, the lake and the great English trees.

'*Fortuna*?' said Nan. 'Why did you think of that place?'

'No reason. I was just remembering how you went to work there. What was it like, Nan?'

'I can barely remember it. A great cold kitchen, as big as our whole upstairs it was, and dark, and, oh!' she flung her hands up in the air, 'Rooms, Ruth! Endless hallways of them, upstairs and down, rooms, rooms, rooms, all for us girls to clean!'

'And the garden?'

'I hardly saw it.'

'But you were living there!'

'Working there,' corrected Margaret May.

'And after that you got married.'

'Yes.' Margaret May half turned her face, so Ruth couldn't see her expression. An image of Don Gower had strode into her mind: handsome Don Gower on the day she'd first met him, standing at *Fortuna's* kitchen door, the big box of groceries hoisted on his shoulder, looking down at her. 'Here, let me do that,' he'd said, when she'd gone to take the box from him, and she'd watched his shapely fingers arranging the jars and packets on the kitchen table, felt the warmth from his body as she stood beside him. After all these years it still gave her a whip of fury to remember how she'd burned for him.

'Nan? What's the matter?'

'Nothing.' Margaret May fought hard for a smile. 'Just a goose walked over my grave.'

'Oh, *don't*!' Ruth grabbed at her grandmother's hand. 'Don't *say* that!'

'It's just an expression,' said Margaret May. 'Have you ever seen a goose in Barinjii?' She rose from the bench in a single fluid movement. 'You'll have a different life from me,' she told the girl firmly, 'a different life altogether.' She nodded and handed the letter back. 'Here, you take care of that while I get on with my watering.'

26

'Let me help.' Ruth jumped up and reached for the watering can.

'No need,' said Margaret May, taking it from her, and Ruth felt that in this small gesture Nan was closing a door on her, gently but firmly, sending her away.

'Please let me carry it,' she pleaded.

'There's no need, it's empty,' said Margaret May. 'I can manage.' She twirled the big can from her hand. 'Light as a feather, see?'

four

On this beautiful morning Father Joseph was also out in his garden, his shabby black cassock moving amongst the rows of tomato plants. Back home in Ballyroan he hadn't seen a tomato till he was ten years old, that blessed day he'd run a message for Mrs Stavely at the White Stag Hotel and she'd given him threepence and a round red fruit he'd thought was some kind of plum. He'd bitten right into it and the juice had spurted down his chin and he thought he'd never tasted anything so grand – like eating a bit of sunshine, a warm summer's day on your tongue. The next time he'd got hold of a tomato had been in the seminary: a whole basket full of them left on the steps by some kind soul.

Two tomatoes in ten years! And now he had a whole garden full of them, all types and sizes: Harbingers, Cardinal Kings, Ruby Queens. The Harbingers were at their peak: the old man parted the leaves of a healthy bush and found a great plump beauty, so ripe it was, so ready, that the moment he cupped his hand beneath it, the fruit fell from its stem into his palm. He sniffed the perfume of its skin and dropped it gently into his pocket – with some of Mrs Ryan's bread, a dab of fresh butter, black pepper and a few leaves of Maidie's fresh basil he'd have a feast fit for a king!

He bent to pick up his gardening fork and then straightened again. A young girl was running across the paddock outside his back fence. It took him a moment to recognise that the girl was Maidie's little granddaughter. Ruth, she was called.

Only she wasn't so little now. His old eyes widened, he was astonished by the size of her. Why, she was almost a young woman! 'Ruth,' he called. 'Ruth Gower! Come over here a minute!' He hadn't seen that one in church for a long, long while. 'Ruthie!'

The girl kept on running. 'Can't stop! Something I have to do!' she flung back over her shoulder into a mass of wild brown hair.

The old man returned to his tomatoes. 'She'll keep,' he muttered, reaching for the fork again. But as he dug the prongs into the rich crumbly earth a frown deepened across his broad forehead. 'Aaw,' he breathed, recalling how Maidie had got the idea in her head that the girl would be going to the university down in Sydney. Sydney University! That sink of iniquity – hardly a week went by that you didn't come across some scandal about the place written up in the newspapers. He needed to talk to Maidie, get some sense into her, and the girl too, if that was possible.

And then his big face cleared – ah, it would be all right. The girl didn't stand a chance of winning that scholarship, not with competition from every high school in the state, and from the great private schools in Sydney: Ignatius and Riverview, Saint Joseph's! With boys from those grand places, boys from the rich old families, how could a girl like Ruth Gower, a shop-keeper's daughter from a little place like Barinjii, ever stand a chance? The whole thing was a daydream; Maidie had always been a bit of a daydreamer, her nose in a book whenever she could get hold of one, and from all he'd heard, the girl was very likely the same. But daydreams fade and she'd get married like all the rest of them. She'd have a family and settle down.

From the house behind him came the faint, aching shrill of the telephone and Father Joseph's large foot went still on the edge of the fork. He waited, chin lifted, eyes narrowed, like a big rough dog scenting trouble in the wind.

The ringing stopped. He pictured his housekeeper, Mrs Ryan, in the hallway, the receiver held close to her ear.

At this time of the morning it would be Tom Lester again, for sure, ringing about his daughter Ellie, wanting to know whether Father Joseph had spoken to the Finn boy. As if you could speak to that one! As if you could do anything! Nothing short of exorcism would do for that young devil! Father Joseph waited for the squeal of the screen door and Mrs Ryan's voice calling, 'Phone call for you, Father!'

There was nothing. One of Mrs Ryan's cronies ringing for a bit of a natter, he decided, relief surging through his hard old veins, and set to work with the fork again.

He'd spoken to the boy last night, and he'd had to drive all the way over to *Fortuna* to do it; the boy wouldn't come to him. He could tell from the expression on old Mrs Finn's face when she saw him in the hallway that he wasn't welcome. The old lady was the boy's grandmother; young Mrs Finn had run off when Tam was only small.

That boy! Father Joseph had waited a full twenty minutes, cooling his heels in the long gloomy room they called a library before Tam had come sauntering in. 'You wanted something, Father?' he'd asked insolently, and Father Joseph had said his piece while the boy sat perched on the edge of the huge mahogany table, legs swinging, answering to no one, least of all the parish priest. 'Will that be all then?' he'd said at last, and sauntered out again, whistling.

The tune had sounded familiar, it had got into the old priest's head; he'd been halfway home along the bumpy road before he'd realised that the boy had actually been whistling a hymn. 'Cradling Children in his Arm', it had been. The words were still playing over in his head:

Cradling children in his arm,
Jesus gave his blessing.
To our babes a welcome warm—

The insolence of the boy took your breath away. The sheer hide of it, whistling hymns about the good Lord cradling children in his arms, when Tam Finn had got half the girls in the district in the family way! There'd be no father to cradle those poor babes!

The boy's own father was away on business in Sydney; but even if Harry Finn had been at home, the old priest knew he'd get nothing out of him: he'd been the same in his own young days. You were powerless with people like the Finns. Lords of the district! They didn't bloody care! He'd got nothing last year when he'd spoken to him about Mrs Ryan's niece, Kathy.

'Wild oats, Father,' Harry Finn had said. 'Know what they are?'

'But the girl,' Father Joseph had protested, and then stopped, the contemptuous curl of the grazier's lips suggesting that the girls of Barinjii got no more than they deserved. 'Remember Saint Augustine, Father,' Harry Finn had counselled, showing the priest to the door. 'He sowed his oats, eh? Bushels of 'em!'

Father Joseph threw down the fork and rubbed at his aching back. A tiny breeze blew up, warm as a breath, teasing the feathery leaves. There was heat in the day already, and a faint smoky scent which reminded him of the winter peat fires, the long rainy winters of his childhood home. He only had to close his eyes and he was back in Mam's kitchen: the scrubbed wooden table with the teapot and striped jug always in the centre, the smoke-dark wall above the big black stove. He saw his mother's feet in boots, cracked brown leather, one heel worn over, and the hem of her long blue dress, such a deep blue that the colour brought a little ache to his heart. 'Ah, Mammy,' he whispered. 'What use am I at all these days?'

RUTH rushed on over the prickly grass of Larsen's Paddock, skirting the big green cowpats, batting away the small black sticky flies. She knew what old Father Joseph wanted: he'd be after her to go to confession, but she was never going again, and when she got down to Sydney she was never going to church either – she only went now, *sometimes*, because of Nan. At the top of a small rise, where the long grass gave way suddenly to bare stony ground, she stopped, gathering up her skirt to pick off the clusters of small brown burrs that had stuck to its hem. She glanced up at the great blue emptiness of the sky: as if some old man was sitting up there, watching you, checking up on your sins! There was only an old man down here, sitting in a stuffy box on Saturday afternoons, where you could smell the tobacco off him, and mould, and sometimes even a whiff of the chook manure he used on his tomato plants.

People wondered what he did in there on those long sad Saturday afternoons when no one came. Ruth knew; she'd peeped round his side of the box one day when she was help-ing Nan with the flowers and there on the narrow seat she'd spied a Superman comic and a half-eaten banana. Superman! She hadn't told anyone because though Father Joseph was an old busybody, he was still her nan's friend, and somehow the comic, crumpled and faded as if he'd found it lying on the road, had made her feel sorry for him. She hadn't even told on him that afternoon when a group of kids had been hang-ing round in the playground and the subject of confession had come up, because the next day was a Saturday.

'What does he *do* in there?' Joey Fenton had asked, and 'What do you *think* he does?' Chris Larsen had replied, and at once a chorus of sniggering had broken out amongst the boys, with pushes and punches and hips thrust out and fingers stuck into the air.

'You mean he's actually *got* one?' Joey Fenton had snorted. 'I thought they cut them off in those places.'

That had brought a fresh round of sniggering, of course.

Brian Geraghty had laughed so hard he'd tumbled to the ground and lay there, pounding his fist in the grass. The girls shook their heads and clicked their tongues; Fee had glanced at Ruth and rolled her eyes.

Iona Malloy had turned pale. Her brother Francis was in the seminary. 'Do they?' she'd whispered, and the boys had fallen silent. 'Do they – do that to them?'

It had been that brief time Tam Finn was at their school. He'd taken no part in the boys' rumpus, only stood on the edge of it, watching. But when Iona spoke he'd come forward and answered her. 'No, they don't, Iona,' he'd said, in such a calm, even voice that you knew what he said was true. 'They don't cut anything. Your brother will be all right, Iona.' Colour had flowed back into Iona's cheeks.

And then Meg Harrison had stepped out from the huddle of girls, walked straight to Tam Finn and touched him on the arm, a gesture so quick, so light, it was hard to believe it had occurred.

Except that it had. Everyone had seen. It was like they'd all been waiting to see.

Tam Finn's face had been expressionless, only his lips had moved slightly, settling into a simple line. He'd shoved his hands into the pockets of his school trousers, turned his back on them and walked out of the yard, away into the paddock and up the hill.

Meg Harrison had followed. They'd watched from the yard as she came alongside him, watched how Tam Finn had reached out and taken her hand, a small act that was without the slightest trace of tenderness; he might have been picking up a knife to peel a new green apple. Tam Finn with Meg beside him turned off onto the track that led to Perry's orchard. Whistles and catcalls rose from the boys then, and poor Kathy Ryan had begun to cry. Perry's orchard, like the little beach beside the creek, was one of the places in Barinjii where couples went to make love, especially in summer, when the grass was long and soft and there was a spicy scent of apples in the air.

MEG Harrison had been married early the next year, though Tam Finn hadn't been the groom. Kathy Ryan had gone down to her aunty's place in Sydney. It was this kind of thing that made the mothers of Barinjii say Tam Finn was bad. And perhaps they were right – except, thought Ruth, it was Meg who'd walked up to him, wasn't it? It was Meg who'd touched his arm. But you couldn't say she was bad, either, or Kathy Ryan, or any of those other girls. They were like small soft birds who'd fallen into some kind of trap, a net woven from the long tender grass and the hot spicy scents of summer and everything that was beautiful on earth. Ruth thought of Father Joseph calling to her across his back fence. He didn't know a thing! It was typical that he never seemed to notice how many baptisms in Barinjii occurred six months after a wedding, and how some of the babies (ones who shouldn't have) had the black curls and rainy grey eyes of Tam Finn.

The sun was higher in the sky now; the day's heat was coming on. A smoky haze made the distant hills shimmer and the air itself had a trembly look, so that you felt you might be able to walk straight through it and find yourself in a different world altogether, like Alice through the looking glass. Ruth smoothed her skirt, ran down the slope and scrambled through the wire fence onto a narrow rutted path. She walked along briskly, arms swinging, hair bouncing against her narrow shoulderblades. It was brown hair, rich and tawny, and her eyes were brown too, and her skin had the golden honey colouring which had been her mum's. 'My nut-brown maid,' Nan used to call her when she was little, sweeping the hairbrush in long gentle strokes, singing,

Ho ro my nut-brown maiden,
Hee ree my nut-brown maiden,
Ho ro ro maiden,
For she's the maid for me.

She'd been small for her age right up till she'd turned sixteen, when her body had begun to develop the kind of gentle rounded shape which made the men standing outside the pub or the post office turn suddenly quiet when she walked past. Occasionally one of them would whistle, after she'd gone by. Ruth ignored them.

'Never look,' Fee had counselled her. 'Never say anything. Pretend you don't hear. Pretend you're deaf and dumb. Unless it's someone you fancy, that is.'

'There's no one,' Ruth had replied.

'That's true,' Fee had replied serenely. 'There's no one here would suit you.' She'd smiled. 'You really *will* have to go to Sydney, won't you?'

It was true, probably, thought Ruth. She couldn't imagine being married to someone like Joey Fenton or Chris Larsen or Brian Geraghty. She couldn't imagine being married at all. Her future seemed unimaginable, despite the letter from the university. In the accident that had killed her mother, Ruth had been thrown clear. 'Thrown clear to have a *life*,' Nan had said all through her childhood, in that low passionate voice which always made Ruth feel uneasy. 'A *special* life, Ruthie.'

Only what if she wasn't special? Ruth walked on along the path. For a while it ran beside a windbreak of tall poplars whose bright leaves flashed with light, and whose long shadows striped the land. Then the windbreak ended and the path went on across a stretch of open land until it reached the crossroads where the Old Western Highway met the Barinjii Road. This was the place where her mother had died. She and Dad had been coming home from a trip to Narromine when their car had hit an unlighted semi on the turn into Barinjii. Her father had been in hospital for two whole months and had come out of it a different person. 'Your dad used to be a laughing kind of boy,' Nan had told Ruth. 'He used to sing – you'd always know when Ray was about because you'd hear the singing.'

Ruth couldn't imagine it. Dad was grey and quiet as a shadow; you forgot about him, you hardly noticed he was there. To think of him laughing was difficult enough, but to imagine him singing was impossible, like trying to imagine a horse crowing, or a big old rooster barking like a dog.

Her mother had simply died, her blood leaking out on the highway long before any ambulance had arrived. Ruth had been a baby in a carry-cot on the back seat. She was strapped in, but the cot hadn't been, and when the semi ploughed in, the cot had sailed out of the open back window onto the verge of the road.

Thrown clear. It did seem special, though in a rather frightening kind of way. She walked out into the middle of the crossroads and stood there quietly. Since they'd built the bypass five years back there was very little traffic; you could stand like that for half an hour without a single car going by, and there wouldn't be a sound except for the wind and the chirp of crickets and the twittering of tiny birds in the long grass of the verges. Ruth closed her eyes and felt the sun on her face and a small warm breeze that teased gently at her hair. She waited.

After a few minutes she sensed her mother come from some other place and stand silently beside her. She could feel her there.

'Do you think that's crazy?' she'd asked Fee. 'Do you think it's crazy that someone would come back from being dead just to see you?'

'No,' Fee had answered. 'No, I don't. She was your mum; of course she'd come back to see you! I'd come back to see you, if anything happened to me.'

'Oh, Fee!'

'I would.' Fee had smiled. 'And I'm not even your mum!'

Ruth reached into the pocket of her skirt and took out

the crested envelope. She opened the flap, drew the two sheets from inside and held them out as if inviting a person standing next to her to read. 'This is the letter from the university, Mum,' she whispered. 'And these are my marks, see? And the scholarship.' She gave a little skip. 'Oh, Mum! I'll be living in Sydney, imagine!'

A bird sang out in the sky. The pages trembled in Ruth's hand, and it seemed to her that beside her on the deserted road there was a small ripple of delight and excitement, of purest, happy glee.

five

With a big box under one arm and the basket of hydrangeas over the other, Margaret May went in through the wooden doors of Saint Columba's. The interior of the church was dim and brown, except for those places where the sun pressed against the high arched windows and its light fell through the jewelled robes of saints and kings and angels.

She walked on down the side aisle, her flat court shoes ringing on the wooden floor which was polished to such a deep shine that Margaret May could see herself reflected there, like a skater on dark ice. She passed the statue of Christ with the briefest of nods, the kind she might give to a stranger who stepped aside to let her go first through a door.

There'd been a similar statue in the chapel at the orphanage, Christ with his arms outspread in blessing, his long face bland and smooth as cream. '*Suf-fer the lit-tle chil-dren,*' the six-year-old Margaret May had read, the words inscribed in gold letters above his head. Those words, together with the outstretched arms, had made her think the man in the long white robe might understand her, she'd thought he might be kind. 'Yes, we do suffer,' she'd whispered, holding out her cracked chilblains for him to see, and the mark on her arm where big Sarah Tyler had got hold of the skin and twisted it right round, and the bruise on her leg that Sister Monica had made. They suffered from the nuns and each other, and some kind of indescribable loss etched deep into their hearts which they could barely understand. There was the crying in the night, too, which Margaret May hated; it sounded like the moaning of the wind in big forgotten trees and it made her think of the grey wolves in the story Sister Barbara had once told them. When the real wind blew and the real trees threw their great black shadows on the barred windows, then the long grey room in which they slept seemed to move as well, sliding forward like a great sled pulled through the snow.

Margaret May had knelt down in front of the statue of the kind man, her hands folded together as the nuns had taught her and prayed and prayed and prayed, 'Please, please, let someone come and take me away!'

But no one had ever come, and in those long cold noisy nights she'd believed that they hadn't come because she'd been bad. She'd prayed to be taken away from the Sisters, and this was bad because the Sisters were good. Of course they were good. Hadn't Mother Evangeline told them that the Sisters were brides of Christ? Christ wouldn't have bad people for his brides, would he?

Only sometimes they didn't seem good: Sister Monica with her sly little pinches and funny smile, *she* wasn't good.

And Sister Therese with her whacky whistly cane, she'd torn out a whole fistful of Noeline Jennings' hair, just for leaning against the wall. How could that be good?

Was she bad to think they weren't good? The thoughts of badness and goodness had chased each other round and round in Margaret May's head, so fast and furiously that sometimes she couldn't get to sleep and she'd climb out of bed and creep down to the chapel and pray to the statue again, 'Please let someone come and take me away.'

Ah, it's a long time ago, thought Margaret May now, though inside her, however old she got, that long grey room seemed as close as ever, as if it was right next door to her own pretty room above the shop and any day she could step down the hall and turn the knob of a door and find herself back in there. 'Ah no,' she whispered, looking down at the little wooden Virgin standing in her corner beneath the long window where Saint Columba sailed in his coracle of wicker-work and hides.

The Virgin was small, only half as tall as Margaret May. She wore a plain straight shift which fell in simple folds about her body and halfway down her bare, slender legs. Her feet were bare too, and her hair hung at her shoulders, plain and straight like the shift. She had no veil or halo, only a wreath of leaves twisted around her forehead. She was young, about Ruth's age, and there was no child.

'Are you sure it's the Virgin?' Margaret May had asked Father Joseph.

'Eh? Who else would it be, out there in that old church?'

'Oh, I don't know. Just any young girl.'

The statue's face had a kind of patient calm, and the square hands curved protectively across the small round belly that pushed against the shift's wooden folds. 'Yes, you're like all of us,' whispered Margaret May, laying the basket of hydrangeas on the end of a pew, opening the cardboard box. Inside were the two big drip-trays she'd borrowed from the shop storeroom; they'd been designed to hold motor oil or paint but they would hold water just as well. She filled the kettle in the kitchen behind the sacristy and poured the water into the trays. The blue hydrangeas floated there, jostling and quivering against each other, and Margaret May gave a tiny gasp of pleasure, because it looked so perfect, exactly as she'd imagined it in her garden this morning: the girl's small brown feet stepping out into a soft blue sea.

There was a sudden rattle at the door behind her, and a strident barking call. 'Yoo hoo! Anyone there?' She turned and saw Merle Hogan had arrived, little Milly Lachlan a few steps behind her, almost hidden by a great green bunch of ivy and ferns. Merle had a sheaf of scarlet gladioli which she held up high in front of her, like a runner bearing the Olympic torch. 'That you over in the corner, Margaret May? What are you doing there?'

'The flowers.'

Merle came clattering up the aisle. 'But it's so dark! How can you see?' Her hand found the switch on the wall and overhead lights came on. 'Ah!' she gasped.

Merle Hogan was a big woman whose flesh seemed to strain from her clothes. Her eyes protruded too, fixing on the blue hydrangeas floating at the statue's feet. 'Whatever's this?'

she cried. 'What've you done, Margaret May? Why are the flowers all over the floor?'

'They're not on the floor.' Margaret May lifted a flower to show the tray beneath.

Merle sucked in her breath. 'Well! What a funny idea!' Her voice rang with astonishment, even outrage. Margaret May was silent. It was one of the things she hated about the little town, how you couldn't do anything the least bit different without being thought 'funny'. You couldn't even think differently, or they would find you out and whisper. For years she had dreaded that her clever granddaughter would have to live that way, but now she wouldn't, and the knowledge almost made her smile.

Merle turned to Milly Lachlan. 'Don't you think it's funny, Milly?'

Milly was Fee's grandmother. She had the same fair skin and wide blue eyes, the same sweet nature, even the same little dimple in her cheek. She hesitated for a moment now, eager to keep the peace, but gazing at the deep blueness of the hydrangeas, she couldn't help herself from exclaiming, 'I think they look lovely!'

'Lovely!' Merle's wide nostrils flared; she hated it when people disagreed with her. She scowled at both of them. 'Someone could get their foot caught and trip! There'd be water everywhere!' When there was no response to this she put her hand on Margaret May's arm and spoke quite softly, as if encouraging reason in a naughty child. 'Don't you think they'd be better in vases, Margaret May? Up on the altar, or on a shelf somewhere?'

Margaret May stood her ground. She knew about people like Merle Hogan. There'd been girls like Merle at the orphanage, big girls, mean spiteful girls, eager to push you around. Hungry girls they were, wanting any little thing you had, or else to make you cry. You got to know them and you learned not to give way to them and make them glad. You recognised them later when you met them in the adult world, angry and hungry still. There was never any kindness in them, not a drop.

Margaret May looked down at her small sea of blue flowers. 'I like them the way they are,' she said. Her voice was quiet, but deep inside she was burning; she wanted to rush at Merle like she used to do with the big bully girls at the orphanage, she wanted to kick at her shins and butt her in the belly, as if the little girl she'd been was still inside her and Margaret May didn't have the heart to drive her away. Living in Barinjii was like living all your life in a school playground. 'Yes, I like them as they are,' she repeated, ignoring Merle's mutinous expression.

Merle stood and stared at her, sharp eyes travelling over the small composed face, which wasn't as wrinkled as it should be, the smart navy dress with the buttons down the front (too good for mucking around with flowers!), the small feet in their plain black court shoes. Always perfectly turned out! She had tickets on herself, all right! Even to go across the street to the post office, Margaret May Gower would wear stockings! And yet she'd come from nothing: come from the orphanage, skivvied out at *Fortuna* till she'd hooked Don Gower from the store. He'd drowned in Skelly's dam one rainy night. Merle had been a kiddie at the time, but she knew there were people in Barinjii who still said that Margaret May had pushed him in. Lots of them said it! And Merle wouldn't put it past her; you only had to look at her face to see she'd be capable of anything, she was that determined.

Milly Lachlan was also thinking of the past. She remembered one long-ago morning when she was a child, how she'd gone to the orphanage with her dad when the nuns had sent a message that their boiler had broken down. Milly had got bored in the basement and wandered up the stairs while he was busy, and then on through the long cold corridors, on and on and on. She hadn't spotted a single soul until, rounding a corner, she'd come upon a tall nun all in brown, putting folded towels away into a cupboard. The nun had turned when she heard Milly's footsteps – and ooh, her *face*! Long and bony like a horse's it had been, only not so kind as a horse. 'Well! Whose little girl are you?' she'd called out, and her voice, like sweetness poured over something bad, had sent Milly running back through all those empty passages and down the stairs to her dad. 'Whose little girl are you?' she'd heard the nun still calling after her.

The thing was, though, Milly *had* been someone's little girl. Margaret May had been no one's.

Imagine that! Imagine being all on your own when you were very tiny – imagine it! Having no one in the whole wide world! When Milly was little her mum and dad had filled up every corner of her universe: if she got scared in the middle of the night then all she had to do was run into their room and climb into the big bed between them and Dad would say sleepily to Mum, 'Hey, Emmie, I think we've got a visitor!

There's someone here!' And while she was snuggling up against them, all nice and warm, Margaret May had been all by herself in that cold dreadful place at the top of the hill. Oh, the pity of it! No wonder Margaret May was so distant, and little Ruth such a quiet child.

'Ruth got her exam results yet?' Merle asked suddenly.

The news of the scholarship was like a five-pound note burning a hole in Margaret May's pocket but she was keeping it to herself for a little while longer. She wanted Father Joseph to be the first to hear. 'I left home before the post,' she lied.

'They'll be coming any day now,' said Merle.

'Yes, I know.'

'She might even get them while you're up here.'

'Yes, she might.'

'Bet she's excited, eh?' Merle stood very close to Margaret May and peered into her face. 'Or worried. Is she worried, your Ruth? Biting her nails?'

'I think she's fairly confident.'

Oh, is she just, thought Merle savagely. 'Ooh, you're going to miss her if she goes away,' she tried, hoping for a bite, the slightest little flicker of misery, but Margaret May only smiled and said, 'Yes, I will.'

'Some kids never know when they're well off, do they? A good home like you and her dad've given her; you think she'd want to stay.'

Margaret May was silent. That got to her all right, thought Merle.

'It's only natural that young people grow up and want to try their wings,' said Milly Lachlan.

47

Or unnatural, thought Merle. Her Helen would never go away.

Margaret May folded the cardboard box and picked up her basket. Merle saw the bunch of basil and thought how that would be for Father Joseph, you could bet on it. He and Margaret May were thick as thieves, and that wasn't natural either. Maidie, he called her. She was his favourite, everybody knew. They went back years – he'd known her at the orphanage when she was a kiddie.

Priests weren't allowed to have favourites, they were supposed to treat everyone the same. But Father Joseph had a special look for Margaret May, his face went soft when she walked in through the door. In her childish heart Merle Hogan thought, It isn't fair.

'You going?' she said.

Margaret May nodded. She didn't tell Merle where she was going or what she was doing this afternoon, like any normal person would. Stuck up. Helen said the granddaughter was just the same. They thought they were too good for you. Too good for Barinjii. Merle watched Margaret May walk down the steps of the church. Trip! she urged her silently, Go on! but Margaret May negotiated the steps with ease and turned onto the path towards the presbytery. Merle put her hands on her hips and wagged her head. 'Off to visit her fancyman,' she observed.

'What was that you said, Merle?' Milly Lachlan called across the aisle.

'Oh, nothing.' She couldn't be fussed to explain. Old Milly wouldn't get it anyway. Merle turned and marched up to the small statue. Father Joseph said he'd found it left behind in some old church, but she reckoned he'd got it from a garbage tip. The wood was a greyish brown, like something you'd find washed up on a riverbank, no colour to it at all. It didn't even look like Our Lady, just some skinny kid in an old nightie with leaves stuck in her hair. And a bun in the oven by the look of it. She glared at the statue for a long moment, like a child in the playground trying to stare someone out, then she nudged the edge of a hydrangea with the blunt toe of her shoe. It bobbed a little on the surface of the water.

'Merle!'

Merle jumped. Milly Lachlan had crept up right behind her. Old stickybeak! Couldn't keep her nose out of other people's business! Geez! She hoped she never got like that when *she* was old. Merle stuck out her foot again and nudged at another hydrangea, just to show she wasn't bothered by the likes of Milly Lachlan. This nudge was harder than the last, the flower rocked violently and drops of water spilled out onto the floor. 'See!' she cried triumphantly. 'I told her there'd be water everywhere! Someone's gonna slip on that!'

'Only because someone else was messing round.'

Merle took an angry breath and said slyly, 'Are there any of those big silver vases empty?'

'No!' said Milly. 'You just leave those hydrangeas where they are!'

Merle shrugged, suddenly tired of the game. 'Have it your own way, then,' she said. 'Only when someone slips and cracks their neck, we'll all know who to blame!'

'There won't be any blame,' said Milly and wandered over

to the other side of the church, flicking her duster here and there, fetching up by the window of the seven wise virgins, staring dreamily around. 'Merle, come over here!' she called.

'What?'

'Just come over here for a moment. Stand where I'm standing.'

'Why should I?'

'I want to show you something.'

'What?'

'You'll find out when you come over,' sang Milly. Light from the window was shining down on her, turning her white hair back to yellow; she was so small that if you hadn't known it was old Milly you might have thought it was a nice child standing there.

Merle flounced over. 'So?'

'Now look over at the statue.'

Merle looked.

'See?' said Milly.

'See what?'

'How the blue hydrangeas look like waves, like she's stepping into the sea.'

Merle put her head on one side. 'It just looks like messy flowers on the floor to me.'

'It's the *sea*. That's what Margaret May would have *meant*.' Milly clasped her hands together. 'She's got such imagination! She always has had, ever since I've known her. She—'

It was too much for Merle. 'Do you know her kids never write to her?' she burst out.

'Eh?'

'*Her kids never write to her!*' bawled Merle.

'What kids? Oh, you mean the older boys? Charlie and Vin? They live in Northern Queensland, I think.'

'And they never come near her, do they?'

'Well, it's a long way to come, isn't it? And you know how it is when you've got a family of your own—'

Merle's eyes gleamed. 'They never write,' she said again.

'How do you know they never write?'

'Joanie Fawkes at the post office told me.'

Milly Lachlan gazed down at the dark shiny floor. After a small silence she said, 'Well, she's still got Ray.'

'Him!' Merle's voice came out too loud. She lowered it, though there was no one in the church except for them, not unless you counted the statues and the saints up in the windows, and Merle didn't – no one could accuse her of superstition. 'You know they say he was dead drunk when he drove their car into that semi out at the crossroads? And killed that poor girl he was married to? Dolly, was it?'

'Polly.'

'Polly, then. Joanie Fawkes says she was only nineteen.'

'Oh, Merle,' protested Milly. 'Of course he wasn't drunk; that's only gossip.' She sighed. 'Poor Ray!'

'Poor Ray!' Merle's voice hissed out contemptuously, and then she began to chant softly, like a naughty child, 'Poor old Ray's a ruin! A ruin, a ruin! Poor old Ray's a ruin, no good to anyone!'

Milly stared at her sadly. 'Oh, Merle,' she said again.

six

Ruth hadn't meant to come to this place when she'd left the crossroads – to the little beach beside the creek – only it was so hot and there was nothing much else to do. It was barely ten o'clock and Fee had told her yesterday that she and Mattie were driving over to Dubbo this morning to buy a birthday present for his mum. 'We're going early before it gets too hot,' she'd said. 'We'll be back by noon. You want to come?'

Two's company, three's a crowd, people said, and it was true. Ruth had known Mattie Howe almost as long as she'd known Fee, but now the two of them were engaged she felt funny being with them, like an extra leg on a chair. Mattie was lovely and said, 'Here's Ruthie!' whenever he saw her at the door, smiling all over his broad freckled face, and meaning it, too, yet she still felt she shouldn't be there. Fee and Mattie had a private world together now; you could hear it in their voices and see it in their eyes and in the graceful movements of their bodies, inclining towards each other: a secret place that was for them alone. There were certain kinds of happiness it wasn't possible to share. So, 'No,' she'd said, when Fee had asked her if she wanted to come with them to Dubbo. 'You two go together.'

'We've got all our lives to be together,' Fee had said, and Mattie had caught a little snatch of her yellow hair in his fingers and tweaked it gently as he echoed softly, '*All* our lives!'

For some reason this had made Ruth want to cry. She'd felt a sudden thickness in her throat and tears welling in her eyes and she'd turned to the window to hide her face from the others. 'Please,' she'd said. 'Please just you two go. I – I've got to do something for Nan, anyway.'

Fee and Mattie had stood in the middle of the room, holding hands, gazing at her silently.

'Please,' she'd begged them, struggling to keep her voice steady.

'But come over later, okay?' Fee had insisted. 'Round noon?'

'Okay,' Ruth had promised shyly, and then Fee had rushed over and given her a hug. 'Oh, Ruthie, Ruthie,' she'd whispered, 'what are we going to do without you when you've gone away?'

Ruth glanced at her watch. It was nowhere near noon. She'd walked away from the crossroads and down the road towards town and then, somehow, though she couldn't actually remember deciding, she'd turned onto the track that wandered along the creek bank and down to the little beach. She'd been sitting here beneath the willows for almost an hour, half waking, half dreaming, caught between two worlds. Sometimes she thought of Sydney and sometimes she thought of Tam Finn, and even when her eyes closed, she was alert to every sound, as if she was waiting for someone. Her gaze drifted slowly to the bank on the other side, to the clump of thick green bushes where yesterday she thought she'd caught a glimpse of his face amongst the shiny leaves. There was nothing there today, no sudden movement, no sound, no blur of pale flesh against the green. Had she really seen him? It was difficult to think of a person like Tam Finn hiding, here or anywhere. He was too bold to hide.

Bold. It was a word you could savour, like a shiny red sweet rolled round inside your cheeks and beneath your tongue. A word that didn't *give*.

The Barinjii mothers whispered endlessly about him round the town. Everyone whispered about him and the whispers, vague and half heard, made him sound like some kind of demon from an old folk story. You could become a story in Barinjii, thought Ruth, you could become what others said about you, while your own self drew back deep inside your skin, deeper and deeper until it became a secret no one could discover.

She felt for the letter in her pocket, drew it out and sat staring at the thick plain envelope, the deep black ink of the letters which spelled out her name. She touched the crest with her fingertip, the jaunty little lion with the bright curly mane, and thought how when the letter had come this morning, Tam Finn had vanished from her mind; he'd hardly seemed real to her. But down here in this shadowy hidden place it was the letter and its promise of a different life which seemed unreal. How could she get on the train and go away from Barinjii, leaving everything behind?

Abruptly she remembered something. One day in those months when Tam Finn had been at their school, Ruth had walked past his desk on the way to hers and his hand had been lying there, the fingers spread, long fingers, narrow at the top, wider at the base where the springy black hairs grew. And the thought had come to her that if the back of his hand brushed against your skin you'd feel every one of those coarse, wiry hairs – and then her blood had surged in secret places and her legs had felt weak and Tam Finn had looked up and grinned mockingly as if he'd read those thoughts. The memory was so vivid it could have come from last week instead of more than a year ago.

She looked over at the bushes again. Everything had gone quiet, even the trickle of water running in the creek seemed to make no sound. Something soft and warm fell on her face. 'Ah!' she gasped, batting at her cheek, but it was only a raindrop – in the shelter of the trees she hadn't noticed how the sky had clouded over. All at once this place she'd known since childhood seemed horrible to her: the drooping willows, the slow brown water, the thick fleshy leaves of the bushes on the other bank, the faint lingering smell of something rotting unseen. She jumped to her feet and scrambled up the bank onto the track, where she stood for a moment breathing in the scent of earth and rain, brushing the damp clinging sand from her skin and clothes. Another big drop of rain fell on her hand. It was a pinkish colour, big as a two-shilling piece, and she stared at it for a moment before raising her hand and licking the drop away. It left on her tongue the faint familiar taste of the dust of the western plains.

A crow swooped down onto the weedy verge and stood regarding her intently with its round white-ringed eye. It was huge, big as a cat, its feathers the same bold blue-black as Tam Finn's hair. She remembered how in some fairytales the witches had familiars: if Tam Finn was a witch then his familiar would be a crow. The intensity of the bird's stare was unnerving, and she wondered what kind of world lay behind that blank round eye: great skies, she thought, and the brown land beneath them, and down below a small huddle of grey fleece, its soft parts ripe for tearing—

The bird took a step towards her. 'Shoo!' she cried. 'Get away!' and it rose into the air on great slow beating wings.

Still it was too early to go to Fee's place. She began to walk slowly in the direction of the town. The road was empty and the paddocks were empty and the only sound was the faint echo of her feet on the hard clay and a dry shushing as the wind blew through the dry stalks of the grass. Far off a crow called, perhaps the very same crow that had stared at her so avidly, but when she looked up the sky was empty too. Yet as she walked on through the empty landscape Ruth had a sense of someone, some watching human presence very near. When she looked round there was no one, but when she walked on she felt it again, like breathing in the air.

And then the whistling began, high and clear and strangely familiar. She walked faster and almost at once she recognised the whistler's tune: it was one of the hymns they sang in church on Sundays, *Come down, O love divine, Seek now this heart of mine*— She swung round and the whistling stopped and once again there was no sign of anyone and no sound except the shushing grass and the eerie pattering of the big raindrops on the leaves of the trees. She started to run and the whistling began again, only now it seemed to come from the side of her, down the bank, somewhere along the creek. The whistler's notes were perfect, clear and true, and somehow this seemed more frightening than anything.

She left the road and ran into the paddock on the other side, and then on into another paddock and then another, scrambling through fences, the dry grass prickling at her legs, and at last onto a narrow unfamiliar track which doubled back and then straightened out and then curved round again. It was a landscape that she didn't recognise at first, but as she ran on it began to become familiar, like a place you've known and haven't seen for a long, long while: the narrow road with a stretch of whispering she-oaks, the low, round hill with an old house on top, and below the house, the sly gleam of deep water. When she saw that water Ruth caught her breath and began to tremble. She was in Starlight Lane. She'd come all the way out to Skelly's dam!

She never went near this place. Skelly's dam was where her grandfather had died, slipped one rainy night when he was trying to save a calf, and drowned. She hadn't been here for years and years, not since that time in primary school when Mr Barlow had taken them on a nature walk. She'd felt she would die back then, seeing the dam up there on the hill like a great eye in the middle of the paddock staring down at her, and all the kids giggling because she was so scared she couldn't keep on walking but stood still and trembled in the middle of the track. Then Mr Barlow had started shouting at her and Fee had said, 'Close your eyes, Ruthie,' and held tight to her hand until they'd got safely past.

She'd been nine then; now she was seventeen and knew it was ridiculous to be scared of a place just because something bad had happened there a long, long time ago. She turned her eyes from the dam and walked on quickly down the lane. The person who'd been whistling would be a long way behind now. Down the creek, she told herself, he went down the creek, and the creek was a long way from Starlight Lane. She slowed a little and glanced behind her: the lane stretched long and lonely, empty as the air.

'Ruth,' someone said, and out of the cluster of she-oaks beside the path stepped Tam Finn. He wasn't very tall, no more than medium height, but his body had a kind of density about it – he was solid on the ground. And yet he was thin, too – when the wind flung the cloth of his blue shirt flat against his chest she could see the outline of his ribs. His face was heart-shaped, and above his wide forehead the thick black curls lay coiled and glistening. There was a kind of animal quality about those curls, they made you think of something hidden in a thicket, bright eyed, coiled and spry.

'Ruth,' he said again. Her name on his lips surprised her; she'd have expected him to have forgotten it or never known, and yet in another way his use of it had all the strange familiarity of her dream.

'Oh, it's you,' she said.

A faint glimmer of amusement gleamed in his eyes. He slid his hands into his pockets. 'Found me, eh?' he said.

'What?'

'Come off it,' he said. 'You've been looking for me all morning. Saw me down the creek, yesterday, eh?'

'No! No, I didn't! I haven't been looking for you!'

He didn't say anything. 'I always go down the creek,' she rushed on. 'I like it there, it's quiet—'

'Good place to read,' he said softly. 'Only where's your book, Ruthie?'

Ruthie! No one called her Ruthie, except for Nan and Dad and Fee. And Father Joseph, sometimes. 'It's got nothing to do with you, me being down there!' she cried. 'And I didn't see you like you say I did, so how could I be looking? I—' She stopped, hearing her voice going on like a guilty little kid.

'Didn't even see me, eh?' Tam Finn wagged his head like a person who knew better, and a flash of pure hatred surged up in her, and then died away. His eyes were such a strange, sad colour: a dark shining grey, like the watery light of a rainy morning when you can tell without opening the curtains what it will be like outside.

Abruptly, yet with the most careless grace, he sank down onto the grass beneath the she-oak trees and patted the place beside him. 'C'mon then.'

She stood still, clasping her hands together behind her back, and Tam Finn gazed at her without expression as if after all he didn't care what she did, couldn't be bothered with her, as if inside his head he was a thousand miles away. She thought of the crow, the landscape it saw from its cold eyes—

He studied the grass where he was lying, stroking it idly with one hand. 'Too wet for you, is it?' he said. Slowly, he unbuttoned his blue shirt and laid it on the ground. She tried not to stare at the hard brown chest, at the two lines of wiry black hair which followed the shape of his ribs and then plunged into the waistband of his jeans.

'There you are,' said Tam Finn, patting the blue shirt. He held out his hand to her, and for a moment she wanted to take it and let him pull her down beside him.

Something glittered on his third finger. The ring finger, where Fee wore her engagement ring, the beautiful blue sapphire which had belonged to Mattie's gran. Tam Finn's ring was gold, the kind of gold that made your eyes ache even though it was real. It was a snake, she saw – or rather a serpent, like the one Eve had met in Eden, coiled round, its head swallowing its tail.

He saw her looking. 'Like my ring?'

She shook her head and he stared down at the ring, twisting it this way and that on his finger. 'It's me,' he said.

'What?'

'The ring. The serpent's swallowing himself, see?' He held his hand up, so the snake's red eye gleamed at her. 'Like me.'

'H-how?' she stammered. 'How is it like you?' She was frightened.

'I'm swallowing myself.' He stared into her face. 'I am. All the way down.'

His words made her freeze and she looked away from him, searching the landscape for something safe and ordinary: Mrs Hogan hanging out the washing up there in her yard, someone's dog out hunting in the long grass, a glint from behind that far-off line of trees where a cart full of milk cans might come jolting along the road. There was nothing but the paddocks and the dam, the silent house up there on the hill and the long lane down which no one else would come.

'C'mon,' he said again, and his hand reached towards her again. 'Be nice to me.'

She tossed her head back and he smiled at her. It was the most beautiful smile and she realised she'd never seen Tam Finn smiling before. Not once. It was like a light going on in a darkened room, showing safe and peaceful things: a vase of painted gumnuts on the mantel, an armchair in a flowered pattern, a child seated at the table, colouring in. 'You toss your head back like my peacock does,' he said to her. 'Really proud, like he doesn't want to know me. But I think he does.'

Ruth didn't say anything.

'His name's Dancer,' added Tam Finn, and he smiled at her again. 'Be nice to me, Ruthie.'

'No – no, I can't,' she stammered. 'No, thank you.'

The smile faded and the light went out of his eyes. 'No, *thenk* you,' he said in a mincing voice which mimicked hers, watching mockingly as she began to edge past him with small steps, eyes down, trying not to tread on the edges of the blue shirt. 'No thank you kind sir, is it?' he said, and she felt his eyes on her back, roving up and down. She turned and sneaked a quick glance at him. Big raindrops had begun to fall again and Tam Finn flung his head back and let them fall on his face. He closed his eyes and stuck his red tongue out to catch a drop, then drew it in again with a little sucking sound. 'We could make love in the rain,' he said. 'It's good making love in the rain.' He yawned and stretched luxuriously, closing his eyes, so the raindrops settled on his eyelids and lay there like soft pink pearls. '*The rain is raining all around,*' he recited, '*It falls on field and tree, It rains on the umberellas here, And on the ships at sea.*' He opened his eyes. 'Did you say *umberella* when you were little, Ruthie? I did. "It's *umbrella*, Tam," they'd say. "Speak correctly, you're a big boy now."'

She'd almost got past him when his hand shot out and seized her ankle; the long fingers with the tufts of black hair were strong as iron.

'Let me go!'

Surprisingly, he did. The heat of his fingers melted away from her. It was like loss and the unexpectedness of it made her look down at him. The wind blew and the trees shivered and their shadows fell over his face so that all at once he looked quite different, like an ordinary boy who felt ordinary sadness and could be comforted if you put your arms around him and pressed your lips against the softness of his hair, and she remembered how gentle his voice had sounded that time in the playground when he'd said to Iona Malloy, 'Your brother will be all right.'

The shadows moved and his face changed again and he laughed up at her.

She stopped. 'What?' she whispered. 'What?'

'Oh, nothing.' He waved his hand dismissively. 'Off you go now, little Ruthie.'

'I—' Some person inside her wanted to stay, but Tam Finn waved at her again and she began to walk away. Where the lane turned she looked back and he saw her looking and leaped to his feet. She began to run then, running blindly, half sobbing, and the rain came pouring down and she ran and ran and she could hear him coming after her, and she hated it and yet she loved it too: the running and the rain pouring, and Tam Finn so close behind her she could almost feel his breath upon her skin. But when finally she turned to meet his face, he wasn't there. No one was there. The lane was empty in the hissing rain.

seven

The path to the presbytery took Margaret May past the small graveyard where her husband was buried.

Don Gower's stone was in the new section, second line, third on the right, a plain granite slab with his name and dates. Margaret May knew people in Barinjii thought it 'funny' that there was no more to the inscription, but she honestly hadn't been able to think of any phrase which would be both suitable *and* true.

He'd had the most beautiful eyes, that was all. So soft they'd been, so deep – she'd been knocked all of a heap, opening the kitchen door at *Fortuna* and finding the tall young man with the beautiful eyes gazing down at her. They were eyes you could trust, she'd thought, being a green, skimpy know-nothing girl. 'Here, let me do that,' he'd said when she'd reached out to take the big box of groceries from his arms.

'Here, let me do that.' No one had ever said such a thing to her before.

They'd begun walking out together; it was barely a month before he'd asked her to marry him. She'd thought she'd be safe, married, but it was as though she'd been out wandering in a wilderness and a big storm had come and she'd found a cave where she could shelter and crawled inside, and then a great heavy stone had fallen across the entrance and shut her in. She'd felt no grief when he'd died, only a sense of relief, as if someone had come and lifted the stone away. 'Thank you,' she'd whispered at the funeral, not to God, exactly, but to the earth, the sky, and the great consoling trees.

The truth about Don Gower wasn't hard to find. He was a sulk. Nothing ever pleased him; she'd discovered that almost right away. The first time he'd made love to her, he'd dragged himself from her body and muttered hopelessly towards the ceiling, 'Is that *all*?' He could turn anything to dust; even the birth of their first child had failed to raise a smile. 'That him, eh?' was all he'd said, and after he'd taken himself from the room, his footsteps echoing down the corridor of the cottage hospital, Margaret May had lain in her bed with little Charlie and she couldn't help remembering the christening of Milly Lachlan's first child a month back; how Frank Lachlan had stood in the church with his arm around Milly and the baby and his smile had been like melted gold.

Don could sulk darkly for weeks. He wouldn't answer when you spoke to him; the boys kept out of his way. 'Dad's in a mood,' she'd hear them whisper, scuttling away to their rooms; it didn't seem right that they should have to live like that. Or he'd pick a fight with one of them and then go rushing off into the night. In the early years she'd stayed awake, waiting for him to come back. Later, she slept on. She'd begun to find it hard to say his name, the name which, long ago in the kitchen at *Fortuna*, it had almost stopped her breath to hear.

Don. Like a dead bell tolling.

It had been pouring with rain, that last time he'd rushed off from the house. The creek had flooded for the first time in thirty years, all the dams were brimming – just thinking of that night made her mouth grow dry, and she almost ran past the graveyard, suddenly overcome by a childish fear that he might come back, rise up accusingly from beneath that granite slab, large with forbidding life, or quite simply walk out from behind a tree. There were nights when she couldn't sleep for fear that someone like him might come for Ruth, some big handsome Barinjii boy who knew nothing and wanted to make sure Ruth knew nothing either. Men didn't like it if a girl was clever, and they sensed it right away. It didn't matter if you were tied down with a house and babies, it didn't matter if you never had a moment to yourself, if your life was as thick and stupid as a cow bailed up in a milking pen, leg tied; they didn't like you being clever and you had to pay. She didn't want Ruth to pay.

The path brought Margaret May to the back of the presbytery, where she could see Father Joseph's bulky figure in the garden, forking the earth round his tomato plants. He was the nearest she'd ever come to having a parent, and she loved the old man, though there'd been times when he'd let her down. Like that time way back in the orphanage when she'd given up praying to the statue and complained to him about the nuns. 'Ah, but they're hardworking women, Maidie,' he'd said, 'and they have their sorrows, too.' He'd swept the damp hair from her eyes and then laid his big hand on the top of her head where it had felt like a promise of some kind, but it wasn't enough for her, it couldn't make up for all the cold nights and the pinching and pushing and the sting of Sister Therese's skinny cane.

'But they're *cruel*!' she'd insisted.

He hadn't answered.

'Father?' she'd whispered, tugging at his sleeve. 'Father Joseph?'

'Sorrow can make us all cruel, Maidie,' he'd said at last.

She'd stamped her foot. 'But they're *nuns*!'

On and on he'd gone, then, as if he'd been addressing a whole churchful of people instead of one small, unhappy girl. 'Ah, the sorrows and the cruelties of this world, Maidie, they make us what we are. That's why we must always try to be kind to others, see? Like the good Lord was kind.'

'He wasn't kind to *me*!' she'd bawled, remembering the statue in the chapel, the endless, useless prayers.

She'd been eight at the time. Later on, when she was fourteen, he'd found her the job at *Fortuna*. He'd driven her over to the property himself – his horse, she remembered suddenly, had been called Patrick. Father Joseph would have been quite young then: black hair came to mind, and ruddy cheeks, and a way he had of running up the broad stone steps of the convent, taking them two at a time.

Now he was old, and old-fashioned too. She longed for him to share her joy at Ruth's good fortune, but she knew he still believed that a woman's place was in the home. He hadn't said much when she'd told him about her hopes for the scholarship, but she suspected this might be because he'd thought Ruth hadn't stood a chance of getting one, and she felt a little stab of anger for the way a clever girl had to prove herself over and over again.

'Father!' she called, and the old man turned and saw her and his big craggy face was like a shadowy country lit up by the sun.

'Maidie?'

She burst out with it straight away. 'The letter's come!' Her voice trembled with triumph and joy. 'Ruth's got the scholarship! She'll be going down to Sydney in a couple of weeks!'

She watched his face change, the light go out of it, the furrows deepening between his brows. 'She has?' he said, and she could see him struggling to take it in: how a girl could have won this glittering prize and what might happen to her now. A breeze blew up and the leaves of the tomato plants swayed and a few big drops of rain fell.

'It's the greatest chance for her!' said Margaret May.

'The greatest chance?'

'She'll have a life!'

Father Joseph sighed. He leaned forward and touched her lightly on the arm, an arm still so slender that his big fingers could easily have encircled it. 'Margaret May,' he said, and his use of her formal name seemed to sound a warning, 'shall we go inside to the study then, and have a little chat?'

THE study, dimly lit from one small window, crowded with ponderous old furniture, made her feel weak and suffocated. It was in this very room that she and Don had sat to discuss the arrangements for their wedding, and except for the layers of dust and old newspapers, it seemed unchanged. Before she could stop herself, Margaret May had taken the very chair she'd sat on all those years back, and Father Joseph had settled into his. The third, Don's chair, was piled with books and yellowing notes and a scattering of junk mail.

The old priest folded his hands in his lap. 'You'll never be letting her go to that place, Maidie?'

Margaret May's lips tightened. 'You mean the university?'

'I do.'

'Of course I'll let her go.'

There was a silence. Father Joseph bent and flicked at a dead leaf which had attached itself to the hem of his cassock. When he straightened up again his voice was distant – she might have been any old sinner. 'Have you considered the teachers' college for Ruth, Margaret May? Just down the road from Dubbo there? Why, she could board during the week and come home at weekends. You'd have her by you still.'

'I love Ruth more than anything in this world,' said Margaret May. 'You know that, Father. She's the joy of my life, but I don't want to limit her by having her stay with me, I don't want to imprison her. Teachers' college is all very well, but the *university*, it's such a great chance for her!'

'A chance for *what*?' The last word came so fiercely that the newspapers fluttered on the empty chair and in the new silence which followed they were both aware of the shuffle of slippers outside the study, of Mrs Ryan listening at the door.

Father Joseph cleared his throat loudly and then waited while the shuffling faded away down the hall. He said more softly, 'It's a sink of iniquity down there.'

'Iniquity?'

'Sin! That place, your *university*, is fit for Sodom and Gomorrah!' He leaned towards her. 'Only the other day I was reading how there's teachers at that place who advocate free love! Who corrupt young minds, who think nothing of, ah, sleeping with the young girl students, of, of—' he spluttered, struggling to get out the word, '*ruining* them, Margaret May!' He drew a big chequered hanky from his pocket, and scrubbed at his brow, all the while staring at her angrily, eyes popping, as if in her desire for Ruth to have a life she was somehow part of this iniquity.

'I—' she began, but he waved her words away.

'Margaret May, do you know they have a thing down there for these poor ruined girls, a thing called the Abortion Car, and how twice a week it goes round the city, gathering them up, taking them to the doctors' surgeries?'

Down in Sydney, the Abortion Car had long since ceased to function, but Father Joseph had no idea of this: in his old mind its sinister black shape cruised the wicked streets of the city for all eternity.

Colour flooded into Margaret May's face, a tide of anger that he could only think of her clever granddaughter's success in terms of aborted motherhood.

'My Ruth won't be in any Abortion Car,' she told him coldly. 'She's got her wits about her.'

'Wits mightn't be enough.'

His words made her flinch, brought a cold flutter of recognition to the pit of her stomach: recalling how her own wits had turned to jelly when she'd seen Don Gower standing at

Fortuna's kitchen door. 'They'll do to be going on with,' she said.

The old man shook his head and stared down at the floor. 'She'll lose her faith for sure,' he said sadly.

She ignored this. 'I want Ruth to have a profession, Father. I want her to get the best education possible. I want her to be able to provide for herself, come what may.'

The priest leaned back in his chair and his voice turned suddenly jovial. 'It's some fine fellow who'll be coming along for your Ruth, Maidie! Some fine Catholic boy who'll give her a home and family – and isn't home and family enough for any good Catholic girl?'

Margaret May felt a flicker of hatred for her old friend in his big leather chair. How could he talk like this when he knew what had gone on with her and Don? And in other families round here? He'd seen the bruises, the black, punched eyes beneath the Sunday hats – he heard confessions, didn't he? Had his own wits been frozen over there in Ireland, long ago, when he was a poor grateful boy in the seminary? Could he never learn a new thing? With a small angry movement she turned from the sight of him and gazed through the small window at the dark side passage, thinking of her own marriage, the endless tedium: lighting the stove in the morning, crossing the dark yard to the woodpile, the copper boiling, cold washing flapping on the line, the children coming, Don and his furious silences. Closed up with him in the house: in winter the rain like a steel shutter at the windows, in summer the sun like a sword at the door. And this was the kind of existence he would wish on Ruth!

She'd never been anywhere and yet when she was a child in the orphanage she'd look out the window at the full moon riding in the sky and felt absolutely certain that one day she'd see every marvellous place in the world, that one day she'd find the real true thing.

As if he had read her mind, the old man rumbled, 'Are you sure it's not you doing all the wanting, Margaret May?'

Wanting. With startling clarity she saw Don's wrist, the triumphant flick of it, turning the knob of the radio away from the broadcast of *Romeo and Juliet* that she'd been waiting for all week, ever since she'd seen it advertised in the radio programme. They'd done the play at school, she'd loved it; she could still hear Sister Anselm reciting in her beautiful clear voice, '*My child is yet a stranger in the world* —' How those words had struck her then, when she was young. It was how she'd felt, always – a stranger in the world.

The night of the programme she'd got the kids to bed early – they were still little then – and settled down to listen to the radio in the kitchen. The play had got no further than Juliet begging her mother to delay the marriage, when Don had come up from the storeroom and stalked in through the door. 'What's this?'

'It – it's a play. It's *Romeo and Juliet*.'

'Bloody snobs' rubbish!'

Flick. Tinny dance music had filled the room. 'There, that's better,' he'd said.

She'd never bothered to check through the radio programme again.

After a while you stopped wanting things. She didn't want Ruth ever to stop wanting things.

'Maidie?' the old priest was saying.

'I want Ruth to have a profession,' she repeated stubbornly.

He shifted in his chair, leaned forward to her again. 'But don't you see, Maidie, how it makes the man feel shamed when the wife has a job outside the house? People think he can't support his wife and family, they talk.'

'People will talk about anything.'

'Ah—' he spread his hands in sympathy, 'but it makes him feel useless, Maidie.'

'The more fool him!' she cried. They glared at each other. 'I want her to get away from all that!'

The priest exploded. 'Did Our Blessed Lady want to get away?' he demanded. 'Did Our Lady's mother, the blessed Saint Anne, want her daughter to have a profession? And yet the angel came to Mary, uneducated as she was, and she bore a child, and wasn't that child our dear Lord Jesus, the light of all the world?'

Somewhere in the house the telephone was ringing. Father Joseph stopped shouting and listened. The shrilling ceased, and in the silence that followed they both heard the house-keeper's voice saying, 'Saint Columba's Presbytery, Mrs Ryan speaking.' Then there was another small silence in which they both heard footsteps approaching down the hall. A tap on the door.

'Come in,' roared Father Joseph. The door opened and Mrs Ryan's pink face, timid as a sugar mouse, peered round.

She frowned at Margaret May and turned towards the priest. 'That was Mr Lester on the phone, Father.'

'Yes, yes,' said Father Joseph impatiently. 'Tell him I'll call him back later, would you, Mrs Ryan?'

'He wants to know if you've spoken to the boy.'

Father Joseph shifted his weight in the chair. 'Tell him I have.'

'Yes, Father. And would you be wanting tea?'

'Maidie?' he asked, and Mrs Ryan gave the visitor another frown.

'No, thank you,' said Margaret May.

'And you, Father?' the housekeeper persisted.

'No thank you, Mrs Ryan.'

When the door had closed behind the housekeeper Margaret May said in a low, passionate voice, 'So this is your kindness!'

He looked bewildered. 'Eh?'

'When I was little, at the orphanage, there was this day I told you the nuns were cruel to us—'

'You were a *child*!' He waved his hand dismissively, but she refused to be put off in this way.

'You said sorrow makes us cruel, and that one should always try to have kindness in this world.'

'You've a memory on you like an elephant, Maidie.'

'I'm glad of it,' she said. 'It helps when you're trying to work things out.' She leaned forward. 'So do think spoiling a young girl's great chance in life is kindness, Father Joseph?'

He was ready for her. 'It's kindness all right, Margaret

May, for I'm not spoiling the girl's chances, I'm trying to prevent her *being* spoiled.'

She rose from her chair. '*I* was spoiled,' she said bitterly. 'I was spoiled, Father, and it wasn't education or Sydney University that spoiled me.' She picked up her basket and walked out of the study, straight down the hall.

Mrs Ryan was dusting the statue of Saint Peter that stood by the front door. She glanced up avidly as Margaret May swept past.

Father Joseph walked out of the study. 'Margaret May!' he called, and then more softly, 'Maidie.'

The old name got to her. She turned. He was standing there rubbing his hands together, and the rasp of his dry skin was the only sound in the hall. 'The good Sisters,' he said placatingly, 'the ones you mentioned back in there, from the old place—'

'What of them?'

'Do you know where the poor souls are buried, Maidie?'

She shook her neat head.

'Way out the back of Ivanhoe, that's where. Ah, it's a terrible spot, Maidie! Not a tree in sight, the wind blowing, and the dust and sand, and those big old tumbleweeds careening across the graveyard like imps loosed out from Hell. You wouldn't wish a resting place like that on any poor soul.'

There was something strangely beseeching in his voice, as if he wanted her pity, not for those long-dead Sisters, but for himself.

'I'm sorry for them,' said Margaret May. Glancing down at her basket, she noticed the bunch of basil still there, and held it out to Mrs Ryan. 'It's some fresh basil for Father Joseph's tomatoes,' she said.

Sensing forgiveness, the priest's face lit up with a smile. 'Your basil and my tomatoes, Maidie!' he exclaimed, rubbing his hands again. 'A feast fit for a king!'

Over the distance of the hallway, Margaret May looked her old friend straight in the eye. 'My Ruthie's going to Sydney University,' she told him, 'and there's nothing you can say will change our minds!' Her voice rang strong and confident, but as she went down the path and out through the front gate a sense of loss gathered in her heart and seemed to fill the very air she breathed, so that sudden tears came welling in her eyes.

eight

When Ruth arrived at Fee's house a little after twelve there was no one at home; Fee hadn't got back from Dubbo, and her mother was out as well. The rain was gone and the sun was blazing; her damp hair and clothes had dried but she could feel the sticky tear tracks on her cheeks. She hurried round to the garden tap to wash her face, then kicked off her sandals and sat on the edge of the verandah to wait, swinging her feet in the ferns below and humming the melody of Tam Finn's hymn which had crept inside her head.

Tam Finn. A small sudden sob jumped up from her throat. 'Oh, shut up,' she told herself angrily. He'd been teasing her, that was all. Playing with her; spreading his blue shirt on the ground to keep her from the damp, reaching his hand out, seizing her ankle and then letting her go, jumping up so she'd think he was coming after her. He hadn't really wanted to come after her. It was – another small sob burst from her – it was humiliating. Ruth looked out along the empty street. All the way here she'd been longing to tell Fee what had happened down in Starlight Lane, but now she was glad there'd been no one at home. When you were upset and started talking to people you sometimes told them things you later wished you hadn't: like how, when he'd taken that blue shirt off and beckoned her to lie down with him, secretly she'd wanted to, and when she was running through the rain she'd wanted him to be there right behind her, wanted him to catch her; when she'd turned and found the lane empty her heart had dropped like a stone.

What if Mrs Lachlan had been home and heard them talking? What if Mrs Lachlan had passed on the story to Nan? She had a sudden image of Tam Finn from long ago, a small boy in a white shirt standing between his father and old Mrs Finn in the front pew at Saint Columba's. People had loved him then, the little boy from *Fortuna*; they had smiled when he walked into the church, holding his grandmother's hand. Now they hated him, even those girls who'd gone with him for a little while.

'I hate him, I hate him, *I hate him*!' Meg Harrison had bawled in the washroom at Barinjii High after Tam Finn had dumped her. 'I hate him more than anyone in the whole world! He's got no *heart*! I hope he goes to Hell!'

'Oh, he'll do just fine in Hell,' Helen Hogan had said. 'He'll get on really well with the devil. They're two of a kind, maybe.'

There *was* something a bit scary about Tam Finn – the way he'd talked about the snake ring and how he was swallowing himself had frightened her. And those strange rain-coloured eyes: they gave you this feeling there was another person hidden in there down beneath the rain. But that person wasn't the devil, he was more like a shabby importunate stranger waiting outside a door. She thought of his long fingers twisting the ring, his thinness, when the blue shirt had blown back against his chest—

They shouldn't all hate him. She swallowed, picturing the hatred of Barinjii like a great black wave sweeping after him over the paddocks, engulfing him. Someone should love him. Someone should. Not Helen Hogan, but—

A sudden noisy racket filled the quiet street and she looked up and saw Mattie's old Holden lurching down the road. It shuddered to a stop outside the front gate, engine still revving, because if you turned it off it wouldn't start again. The passenger door flew open and Fee burst out onto the foot-path. 'No, no, no, don't stop! You've got to pick your dad up, remember? Go! Go! Go!' The car roared off again and Fee stood waving and blowing kisses till it disappeared around the corner, trailing clouds of gritty smoke. Then she came racing up the path, yellow hair flying, arms stretched out towards her friend. 'Oh, Ruth! Ruthie! I'm so sorry! We had a flat just outside Dubbo, could you believe?'

'I believe.'

'And then Mattie couldn't get it to start again, not for ages. And the spare's nearly had it, and that wheel's got a bit of a wobble anyway, so we had to drive slowly—' She broke off and peered into her friend's face. 'Are you all right?'

'I'm all right,' said Ruth. 'I haven't been to Dubbo in an old, old Holden.' She got up from the verandah and pushed her hair back, smiling – simply to look at Fee, to see her happiness like sunshine, made her feel better. 'Why did you think I wasn't? All right, I mean.'

'I don't know. For a moment, when I was coming in the gate, I thought you looked sort of—' Fee stepped back for a moment and surveyed her friend again, 'different, like something had happened.'

'Nothing's happened. I went for a walk and got a bit hot, that's all.'

'You're crazy, going walking in this heat.' Fee swung the door open on a long cool hall. 'Let's get inside; you lie down on the sofa like a princess and I'll get you a cold drink.'

'I'm all right, honest,' said Ruth, but already Fee was gone, and from the kitchen came the sounds of the fridge opening and closing, the clink of china against glass; and then a brief silence broken by a small, soft scream. 'Aaah!'

'Fee?' Ruth ran into the kitchen, where Fee was standing in the middle of the floor, a scrap of paper in her hand. Her face was white and the band of gold freckles across the bridge of her nose had gone dark. 'Mum's left me a message,' she said in a low, shaky voice, holding the paper out to Ruth, her eyes wide and round. 'She says – she says they've *come*! Look! They're there!' She pointed to a long white envelope lying on the table.

'The results,' said Ruth. 'Yes, I know.'

'You *know*? Why didn't you *tell* me?'

'I forgot.' It was true. Tam Finn had driven all of that from her mind.

'You forgot!' Fee slapped her forehead. 'I don't believe it! Ruth Gower forgetting about exam results!'

Ruth pointed to the envelope lying on the table. 'Aren't you going to open it?'

Fee did a funny little hopping dance on the tips of her toes. 'No! No, I can't! I can't touch it! You do it, Ruthie, please!'

Ruth picked up the letter from the table. 'Will I open it?'

'Open it,' said Fee.

Taking a small knife from the kitchen drawer, Ruth slid the blade beneath the flap of the envelope. There was a soft ripping sound. She drew out the pages and held them towards Fee, but Fee clasped her hands behind her back and shook her head.

'You're not going to look at it?' said Ruth. 'Ever? You're going to be this old, old lady who tells everyone, "I never knew the results of my final exams . . ."?'

'No, I'm not *that* bad. But you read them for me, okay? My hands are shaking like anything, I couldn't even hold it properly. It doesn't matter what's in there anyway, I'm totally, absolutely sure I've failed.'

'And I'm sure you haven't.'

'Yes, I *have*.' Fee tossed her head and the heavy hair went *flap, flap,* against her shoulderblades. 'And I don't care, really. Stupid old exams!' But then she sighed, and her whole body appeared to falter and fold a little into itself, so that she seemed suddenly smaller. 'Mum and Dad will care, though,' she said. 'And Gran. Gran especially. She says a girl always needs something up her sleeve.'

Ruth scanned the sheets quickly and smiled. 'Well, you've got something up yours.'

'What? *What?*'

'Five Bs and an A. You've passed. Told you.'

Fee unfolded. She was strong and beautiful again. 'What's the A for?'

'History.'

Fee sat down on a chair and covered her face with her hands.

'Are you all right?'

Fee's hands flew away from her face. She was smiling. 'Oh Ruth, I was so sure I'd failed! I never did a stroke of work all year. It was all Mattie, you know. All Mattie and getting engaged and making plans – school just faded away. It seemed stupid to be going there. And yet I passed! I passed anyway! I can't believe it!'

'You're a genius, that's all.'

Fee stretched one leg out and admired her slender brown foot. 'Well, you might just be right. Here, give us!' She snatched the pages from Ruth's hands. '*Look* at all those Bs. Queen of the hive, that's me! Only one poor little A. Guess I'll have to wait till Joanie Fawkes kicks the bucket and apply for her job as postmistress.'

'No need. With five Bs and an A you could go to teachers' college.'

'Teachers' college! Catch *me*! Anyway, they don't take married women in that place, not if you're pregnant, anyway.'

'Are you—?'

Fee laughed. 'Could be, who knows? Anyway, bet I soon will be.'

'Would you be happy if you were?'

'Yes. Oh, *yes*! Mattie's child! And mine!'

All good things come to Fee, thought Ruth, and they came easily and naturally, as if she'd been born for happiness. She felt no jealousy; Fee's happiness came because she fitted in so perfectly with life. 'I'm glad,' she said.

'Oh, Ruth. *Ruth!*' Fee sprang up from her chair. 'Oh, look at me! So full of myself, I haven't asked about *you*. Did you get into university? Did you get a scholarship, Ruthie?'

'Yes.'

'Good!' Fee clapped her hands. 'And top marks, I bet.'

'They were all right.'

'*All right*. Oh, *you!*' Fee shook her head and then said a little mournfully, 'You'll be going away then. You really will. All the way to Sydney.'

'I know. It's sort of hard to believe.'

'Are you scared?'

'A little bit, sometimes.'

'I'd be scared if it was me. I love it here where I've always been – I'm an old stick-in-the-mud, really; I couldn't bear to be in some strange place all on my own where I didn't know anyone and no one knew me. I'm not brave like you.'

'I'm not brave.'

'Yes you are,' said Fee, thinking how Ruth didn't have a mother or any brothers and sisters, and how her dad was sort of – funny, not like a real dad at all. And how people told mean stories about her nan pushing her granddad into Skelly's dam, which Fee's mum said was just gossip and pure Barinjii spite. All these things passed across Fee's face and for a moment made it sad, and when they went back into the

83

living room she picked up the beautiful quilt her Aunty Gwen had sent from America and hugged it to her chest as if she suddenly felt cold. 'It's a marriage quilt,' she said to Ruth, running her hand over the pattern. 'You know, I can't believe things either. I can't believe I'll soon be a married lady – it seems sort of – unreal.'

'Mattie's real.'

'Oh yes, my Mattie!' She added softly, 'One day you'll get married too, Ruthie.'

'I'm not sure I want to,' said Ruth. 'Get married, I mean.'

'Of course you are. Of course you will!' cried Fee, though in her heart she thought that Ruth just might not – and Ruth read this in her friend's face, which was tender and kind, but also a little pitying, and she turned to the window and looked down the long garden where they'd played as children, past the shed and the peppercorn trees to the sagging fence, and beyond the fence to the paddocks and the narrow roads beside them and the little lonely farms. She'd seen that view forever and its sameness had seemed to contain a promise that she'd always be here. It had never really occurred to her that she wouldn't be. And now she was going.

'Ooh, isn't it *glarey*!' Fee dropped the quilt over a chair and yanked down the blind.

'Oh!' gasped Ruth.

'What's the matter?'

'Nothing,' said Ruth, but her face had gone pale, and she stared at the drawn blind as if a magician had clapped his hands and made the backyard and the country beyond it disappear. There, it was gone! All gone. All of it. It could happen so quickly, she thought: the blink of an eye, and a world which had seemed part of you forever could be left behind.

nine

Merle Hogan couldn't get to sleep. She turned this way and that way, punching the pillow with her fists, but it was no use. Her head was buzzing.

After leaving Saint Columba's that morning she'd popped into the post office to have a chat with Joanie Fawkes. Joanie had told her that the Leaving Certificate results had been sent out first thing this morning and that Ruth Gower had won a scholarship to Sydney University.

'Sydney University? A scholarship?'

'It's a thing that pays for all their fees and what-have-you – books, fares, lodgings in some fancy college—'

'I know what a scholarship is, thank you, Joanie.'

Merle was ropeable. The hide of that Gower girl! Off to Sydney, to the bloody university, who did she think she was! And the thing that had really got her going was how Margaret May had been in the church with them this morning, messing the place about with her hydrangeas, and she hadn't said a word! Even when Merle had asked if Ruth's results had come, she'd pretended she didn't know. Of course she'd known!

Merle pictured Margaret May in her neat navy dress with the buttons down the front and remembered how there'd been this little smirk on her face: like the cat that got the cream! She hadn't said a word because she thought Merle and old Milly Lachlan weren't good enough to hear!

'Sydney Uni!' Joanie Fawkes had sighed dreamily from behind the post office counter. 'Imagine! It's like a fairy story or something, isn't it? Like Cinderella!'

Bugger Cinderella!

'WELL, what did you expect?' Merle's daughter Helen demanded when her mother passed on the news. 'Where else would a stuck-up teacher's pet like her go to, Mum? No one would want her up here, would they? She'd be an old maid for sure! But, Jesus wept!' Helen cried, swishing her long black hair so that two dead leaves and a few blades of grass released themselves and drifted to the floor. 'I'm sorry for those poor boys down in Sydney!'

'Helen!'

'What?'

'Don't say that!'

'What?'

'Don't say, "Jesus wept!"'

'Dad says it all the time.' Helen chewed on a torn fingernail and added, 'But yeah, I'm sorry for those Sydney boys all right; she won't even give them a sniff!'

'Helen! Go to your—'

'Room!' bellowed Helen before Merle could finish her sentence. 'S'all right, Mum, you can save your breath; I was going anyway!'

Merle was at the end of her tether with Helen. The little madam had started sneaking out at night. Merle hadn't actually caught her in the act, but she was certain of it; she had a nose for that kind of thing. And sneaking out at night in a place like Birinjii could only have one meaning.

All the same, Helen was spot on about Ruth Gower. Boys, even those with a bit of education behind them, weren't keen on that type of swotty girl, and who could blame them? Merle had delivered herself of this opinion to everyone she'd met on her way home through the streets of Barinjii, and there hadn't been a soul who'd disagreed. Boys wanted girls who had a normal interest in a home and kiddies, and you couldn't run a home with your nose stuck in a book all day. Try as she might, Merle couldn't imagine that little snip Ruth Gower changing nappies or wiping up puke in the middle of the night; she couldn't imagine her comforting a man. No more than she could imagine Margaret May doing any comforting, even though she'd had three boys before Don Gower died.

Before she'd pushed him in the dam.

Merle gripped her pillow and wrung it with both hands – Margaret May Gower had done her hubby in for sure! What had he been doing, anyway, wandering round the country in the middle of a rainy winter's night? Some people said there was madness in his family, like there was in the Finns', but Merle didn't believe a word of it. Don Gower would have been out wandering because Margaret May had driven him from the house with her nagging, because he couldn't stand the sight and sound of her for one minute longer and preferred to be out in the rain. And then Margaret May would have gone sneaking out after him . . .

Don Gower had been a big man – Merle could remember him from when she was a girl, hulking behind the counter at the store; she'd thought he was an ogre. Margaret May was little and light and so soft spoken you'd think butter wouldn't melt in her mouth – but that didn't mean she couldn't have finished him off! In the dark and with the ground all slippery with mud, and the rain pouring down so he couldn't hear a sound behind him – just one push would do it, one shove in the back and he'd be gone. Skelly's dam was a deathtrap – it was still a deathtrap now: the sides had eroded into steep banks, sheep and cows and wild animals were always going in.

And look how she'd gone for the priest, instead of to the police like she ought to have done, like anyone else would do! She'd wanted Father Joseph to help her cover things up, and he would have, you could bet on it. They were close, the pair of them; always had been. Too close. Merle could remember from the time she was pregnant with Helen, going over to Benson's place for a pot of honey and seeing the two of them walking along the road near Perry's orchard; they'd been so close together they could have been holding hands. Margaret May had been wearing a white dress with green flowers printed on it, far too good for traipsing round the dusty back roads of Barinjii. People said Father Joseph had made that fancy garden for her too, not long after Don Gower had died – and

Margaret May was always over at the presbytery. They were old now, of course, but they hadn't been all that old the time she'd seen them out walking together. Where had they been going? Or coming from? Perry's orchard? She sniggered at the thought of it. Or perhaps they'd been off to the little beach down the creek!

Merle was on a roll. Suddenly she remembered Vinny Gower. Vinny was Margaret May's second son; Merle had been at school with him. Vinny had been big like Don Gower, but Father Joseph was a big man too. And Vinny had been dark haired, while the other Gower boys had been fair, like Don. Father Joseph had been dark, before his hair went white. And Vinny had those same red cheeks the priest had, and those same big square white teeth. 'Aaa-aah!' breathed Merle with satisfaction. It was as if, on a hot summer's day, she'd been given a bowl of cold red cherries and her fingers were hovering above them while her eyes searched greedily for the biggest, the juiciest, the most luscious one of all – and she'd spotted it, and her fingers went dipping down straight towards their target: *Vinny Gower was probably Father Joseph's son!*

'Len!' she whispered excitedly, nudging at her sleeping husband's side. 'Len!'

Len stirred drowsily. 'What's up?'

'Len, do you remember Vinny Gower?'

'Who?'

'Vinny Gower – Margaret May's second son. He was at school with us.'

'Vin Gower? Sure. Used to play cricket with him down the oval after school.'

'Do you remember what he looked like?'

'Big kid, wasn't he? Black hair. He had those bright red cheeks, like – like—'

Merle's eyes gleamed. 'Like Father Joseph's.'

'Eh?'

'Father Joseph. Don't you think Vinny Gower had a look of Father Joseph about him?'

Len sat upright. 'Jesus wept, Merle!'

'What?'

'Let it be! For pity's sake don't spread stuff like that around!'

'I wasn't going to,' protested Merle.

'Says you.' Len lay down again, pulling the sheet closely round him, as if it might afford some protection from his wife. 'For God's sake, leave the poor devils alone.'

IN her room above the shop, Margaret May couldn't get to sleep either. She lay there thinking that though she'd had many hard times in her life and come through them all, she simply wouldn't be able to bear it if anything stopped Ruth from going to Sydney. And in the room next door to hers, Ruth shifted restlessly while Tam Finn's face and his hands and his voice crowded into her mind and Sydney faded and she simply wasn't sure if she wanted to go away.

OVER at the presbytery, Father Joseph closed his breviary and turned out the light. The room was utterly silent. Outside his windows the country was silent too, so quiet he almost fancied he could hear the sweet sound of his tomatoes ripening, coming into fullness, drawing nourishment from the rich dark soil. Images swam slowly through his mind. He saw the girl running across the paddock this morning, the spitting image of Maidie at that age. He saw Maidie herself appearing at the presbytery door on that terrible winter's night when Don Gower had died, her dress soaked through, her hair all straggled with rain.

'Don's fallen in the dam!' she cried. 'He's drowned! I can't get him out! Help me, please!'

There'd been bruises on her face.

Bruises.

He blotted the image out and the young girl came back, running across the paddock, her hair streaming out in a dark brown cloud. He thought about her going to Sydney. It was a long time since Father Joseph had been to the city, but he remembered it well. Strolling through Hyde Park on his way to the cathedral he'd felt something soft yet solid land squarely in the middle of his back. 'Down with the Pope!' a young voice had shouted from behind him. He'd turned and found a gaggle of students – beards and berets, black turtlenecks, fresh from some demonstration – smirking on the path behind him. Ignore it, he'd thought, and walked on. The missile had been a tomato, of all things, red and pulpy, overripe; it had taken him the best part of half an hour in the men's room to sponge the mess off his best black clerical jacket.

That was the city for you. No respect. A girl like Ruth Gower would be fair game down there, all right. 'Ah, Ruth,' he whispered into the darkness of the room. Ruth among the alien corn.

IN the garden of *Fortuna* Tam Finn wandered down the path towards the lake, hands in his pockets, whistling. The moon came out and turned the water silver and from the dark shrubbery behind him there came a swift patter and a rustling and a sudden, unearthly scream.

The boy knelt down on the path and waited silently and the peacock came up to him and Tam Finn held out his hand to it and gazed into the small, indifferent eyes. 'Hello, Dancer,' he said softly, and the peacock tossed its head back proudly and Tam Finn laughed, remembering Ruth Gower in Starlight Lane. 'Hello, my beauty,' he whispered, 'hello, my lovely one.'

Ten

Ruth took the photograph from the mantelpiece and held it in her hands and her mother's beautiful face smiled up at her, eyes shining, full lips resting lightly one upon the other. Ruth bent her head and kissed the photograph: how cold the glass felt beneath her own warm lips! Her mother had been nineteen when she died, only two years older than Ruth was now.

'Did you ever feel like me?' Ruth whispered. 'Did you ever feel like you wanted something and yet you didn't want it, all at the same time?' It was February now, and Ruth was thinking of her departure for Sydney, only two days away. And thinking, too, of the time she'd met Tam Finn in Starlight Lane: that strange rush of longing and desire, and the fear of that longing that had made her want to run away. There were nights when she woke suddenly in her bed and wished with all her heart that when he'd held his hand out, she'd taken it, that she'd lain down on the grass beside him, on the blue shirt he'd spread out for her.

She'd seen him only once since that morning in Starlight Lane, on a cold evening last week when a southerly had come through and the temperature had dropped from high summer to near winter in less than half an hour. 'I think we'll light the fire,' Nan had said and Ruth went out to the shed to fetch some kindling. The back gate was open, swinging in the wind, and when she'd gone to close it she'd seen Tam Finn away across the paddock, hands in his pockets, kicking an old tin can along the track. In that uneasy twilight, beneath a pink sky with shreds of livid grey cloud racing, he'd looked like an ordinary boy.

She'd closed the gate and gone on watching him. A little further on across the paddock he'd stopped suddenly and flung his head back, and from some deep and hopeless part of him had come a long, low, shivering howl, which made her think of some abandoned creature who'd suddenly glimpsed the crack in the universe which would bring him down. And standing there at the back gate Ruth had realised that even if he'd wanted it, desperately, Tam Finn could never be an ordinary boy.

'She'd be proud of you.'

Ruth swung round, so deeply startled that she almost dropped the photograph. Her father was standing right beside her; she hadn't heard him come into the room. 'What?'

Shyly, he gestured at the photograph. 'Polly,' he said, his voice sounding strange on the name, as if he hadn't spoken it for years. 'She would have been so proud of you, getting that scholarship, going down to Sydney, all that hard work you did for the exams.'

'I didn't,' cried Ruth, flushing scarlet. 'I mean, it didn't seem hard to me.' She remembered the long spring evenings on the bench in Nan's garden, sifting through her notes and books until it had grown too dark to see; her pen flying over the pages in the exams – it was like some special kind of happiness, or the memory of some secret joy.

'You're a clever girl,' said Dad. 'Take after your nan. And your mum, of course. Polly was clever, too.'

'Was she?'

'Oh, yes.' His freckled hands seized at each other, clasping and unclasping. 'If it hadn't been for that old semi, she'd have—' he swallowed, shook his head sadly, 'she'd have done wonders, our Polly.'

Ruth put the photograph carefully back up on the mantelpiece, in its place. When she turned, her dad was gazing raptly at her face. He cleared his throat. 'Give us a kiss,' he said.

There was something about him that made even your lips feel awkward; and the skin of his cheek was as cold as the glass over Polly's face. The thought that all her lost mother's radiance had been directed at this sad man filled Ruth with a kind of desolation.

But he'd been different then, Nan had said; he'd been a laughing, singing kind of boy. It seemed Polly's death had stopped his song.

SHE hurried from the house and made her way to Fee's place, quickening her step as she passed Joanie Fawkes' post office. Yesterday she'd been about to go in there to buy stamps when she'd heard Joanie's voice drifting out through the mesh of the screen door. She'd been talking to Mrs Hogan.

'She'll get her head stuffed full of nonsense that's no use to anyone,' Joanie had been saying.

'Specially not for a girl.'

'Blue-stockings, they called them in my grandma's day. Old maids, all of them.'

'And no wonder. You can't blame the men. Stands to reason girls like that'd know nothing about running a home.'

'Take no notice,' Fee had consoled her later. 'They're jealous, that's all.'

Taking no notice was easier said than done, because Ruth couldn't help thinking, sometimes, what if they were right? What if they were right and all that came from this marvellous new life that Nan kept talking about, was that she ended up an old-maid schoolteacher, all by herself, living in a room in someone else's house, walking along the road in the mornings to some tiny country school? As she passed the familiar shops and houses Ruth felt they had a different air about them, as if they'd already begun to slip away into the past, like photographs of small children stuck into an album. Last night she'd dreamed she was wandering in a strange city, a vast unknown place where each unfamiliar street led into another and she had no place of her own where she could go, so that there was only the walking, on and on and on . . . she'd woken with a horrid jump of the heart and still half asleep, stumbled to the window to check that Barinjii was still outside. Of course it had been, but the homely buildings looked less solid, and their shadows wavered uncertainly beneath the moon. Doubt had played like knucklebones all down her spine and she'd fallen back to sleep with the thought, I don't want to go!

She turned out of Main Street and crossed the small park with its ragged grass and row of scruffy rosebushes planted beside the war memorial. Hopeton Street was on the other side, and today there was no old Holden parked outside her friend's house. Ruth clicked the latch on the gate and began to walk up the path. Fee's bedroom, with its big wide windows, opened onto the verandah. The curtains were flung back and she could see inside, where boxes and packages lay scattered on the floor, and Fee's wedding dress hung in splendour from the rail up on the wall. Her own bridesmaid's dress hung there too, its shadowy lilac colour swallowing up the light. Beside Fee's dress, it looked as dull and insubstantial as a shabby old book beside a vase of shining flowers.

Fee came into the room. She wore shorts and an old tee-shirt and her feet were bare, but floating all around her, from the fair crown of her head to the soles of her grubby bare feet, was a cloud of white lace and tulle.

Fiona Lachlan was trying on her bridal veil. She stood in front of the mirror, fixing the little coronet more firmly round her head, then she grasped two handfuls of lace and tulle and began to dance, and the beautiful veil floated out around her like a great wave of foam that would lift her up and carry her away. Her face wore a dreamy, absorbed expression; she didn't notice her friend standing outside on the path.

Ruth turned and hurried back to the gate. She closed it quietly and then began to run away down the road, up Hartley Lane and out into the paddocks behind the houses, through the fences, along the paths and narrow, dusty roads. She didn't know where she was going or why the vision of Fee in her bridal veil had so disturbed her, only that she had to run, and she ran blindly like she had on that morning when she'd thought Tam Finn was chasing her. The tumult inside her on that day had been a kind of fearful, joyous flood; what she felt now was its very opposite: a slow and aching draining that left only loss behind. Eyes blurred with tears, she stumbled at last down the creek bank and came to the little beach.

Someone was down there.

Someone all covered in blood was lying on the narrow stretch of sand.

'Ah.' Ruth drew in a cold, aching breath, but she didn't scream because her throat had closed on any sound. She simply stood and stared and as she did, her tear-filled eyes began to clear and she saw that the pool of blood was nothing more than a red dress.

A dark-haired girl in a bright red dress was lying on the sand. The girl had one arm across her face but Ruth knew at once who it was. She knew the dress and she knew the dark hair, the deep blue-black of it, like Tam Finn's, like the shine on a crow's wide wing.

Helen Hogan.

Helen lowered her arm, and Ruth saw that her face was swollen and smudged with crying. There was a big rip in her dress almost from waist to knee. Helen sat up and bunched the tear together. 'What do you think you're staring at?' she demanded.

'Nothing.'

'Nothing, eh?' Helen tilted her head back and yawned.

She gathered the blue-black hair in big handfuls, twisted it on top of her head and then let it fall again, heavily. Her red dress was cut low in the front so the tops of her white breasts showed and Ruth imagined Tam Finn's head lying there, his white face pressed into that soft, translucent skin.

'I could do what you did,' said Helen unexpectedly.

'What?'

'Win a scholarship. Go to Sydney.' Seeing the expression on Ruth's face, her voice rose. 'Oh yes, I *could*. Easily. If I wanted to, that is. If I'd wanted to stay at school and sit mooning over dusty old books and writing essays day and night and night and day, I could have passed those exams just as well as you did. And gone down to the *university*.'

'Yes, but—' began Ruth, and then couldn't think of any more to say.

'*Yes, but—*' mimicked Helen, and Ruth remembered Tam Finn mimicking her in Starlight Lane: '*No, thenk you*.' She pictured the two of them, dark heads together, talking about her and laughing.

'*Yes, but*,' said Helen again. 'Yes, I could have, but I wanted to have a life, see? A *real* life. That's the thing, you know; the *only* thing.' With a sudden swift movement she got to her feet and Ruth flinched back from her.

Helen laughed. 'Thought I was goin' to punch you, eh? For coming spying around down here? Well, I'll tell you something for free, Miss High-and-Mighty, I don't hit babies, see?'

There was blood after all, Ruth saw. A thin red trickle of it was sliding down Helen's long, pale leg.

They both gazed at it. Helen made no move to wipe it

off. She swung her head back, and the black hair swirled. 'So just you remember this when you're down in Sydney: just remember that you know nothing, okay? Nothing that's *real*.'

A sudden gust of hot wind sent the long fronds of the willows swaying. 'Something's burning,' said Helen, sniffing at the smoky air. 'Somewhere.' She smiled and now Ruth could smell the burning too, and when she breathed in, she thought there was a taste of ashes in her mouth.

'Scared?' sneered Helen, throwing her arms out wide. 'Scared of fires, little girl? Little *baby*?'

'No, I'm not.'

'Yes you are.' Helen laughed. She threw her head back again, and her beautiful throat quivered with the laughter, a beating pulse beneath the pearly skin. Then she stopped, and her voice was filled with scorn as she looked Ruth up and down. 'Better run home to Mummy, then! Oops!' Helen slapped a hand over her grinning mouth. Her fingernails were painted red to match her dress, but the polish was chipped and the tips were ragged and bitten down. 'Sorry! I forgot, you haven't got a mummy, only a wicked old granny who pushed her hubby in the dam!'

'She didn't!'

'Oh, didn't she? How come everyone says she did, then?'

'It's *not* everyone. It's just people like you.'

'People like me, eh?' Helen smiled dangerously. 'You mean like – the dirt beneath your little feet?'

'No, I didn't mean that, I meant—'

'I don't care what you meant,' said Helen savagely, 'or what you think in that fancy brain of yours, Little Miss Know-

Nothing!' She glanced down at her torn dress, the smear of blood on her thigh, and smiled slowly. Then, dismissively, she waved her hand. 'Get lost, why don't you?' She lunged forward again. 'Go on! Scram! Run away home to Nan!'

eleven

Up at Saint Columba's they were doing the flowers again. In the back kitchen, Milly was taking down the big silver altar vases for the pink lilies Margaret May had brought. Cold water spurted from the tap above the sink, filling the small room with the deep dark scent of foliage and earth.

Merle Hogan's big hands moved angrily amongst the flowers; she'd had another fight with Helen this morning – and now mucky green sap was running, the thick stalks of the lilies were leaking all over her. 'Ugh! Nasty stuff!' She wiped her fingers on the front of her apron and went to stand at the small window which overlooked the presbytery garden. 'Tsk,' she murmured after a little while, and shook her head from side to side. 'Tsk!'

'What's the matter, Merle?' asked Milly.

'Will you look at that poor old man! Just look! Why, he's a shadow of himself!'

Milly went to the window and peered out: she saw Father Joseph forking the soil round his tomato plants and thought he appeared as big and bulky as ever. 'He looks all right to me.'

Merle drew in a loud, important breath and rounded

suddenly on Margaret May. 'I'm surprised at *you*,' she said, 'upsetting him like this!'

'What do you mean?'

'You know very well what I mean! The poor old soul's worried sick about your Ruth swanning off to Sydney and what she'll get up to there!'

'She's not swanning and she's not getting up to anything,' retorted Margaret May. 'She's going to the university to study for her degree.'

'Her *degree*,' sniffed Merle. 'Studying's not all they do in that place! Mrs Ryan told me yesterday the worry about your Ruth is eating the poor man away! And to think you and Father Joseph used to be such *friends*!' Merle's words were accusing but her voice had a gloating sound – this would teach the old fool to have favourites! And it would teach Margaret May Gower a lesson, too.

Margaret May looked out into the garden; the old man's arthritis was troubling him again, she could tell by the way he moved. They hadn't spoken to each other since that morning in the presbytery three weeks ago. She'd believed then that he'd come round to the idea of Ruth going to the university, but he'd stuck to his guns and she'd stuck to hers. They shook hands at the door after Mass, and that was all. It seemed strange that she no longer had him as a friend when they'd known each other for such a long time. When Ruth goes, she thought, when Ruth goes down to the university – when it's an accomplished fact – then he'll come round. Only – Margaret May was worried about her granddaughter. Last night when they were doing the dishes, Ruth had said suddenly, 'Nan, what if—' and then stopped, the tea towel drooping from her hand.

'What if what?'

'Well, down in Sydney, what if people don't like me there?'

'Of course they'll like you!'

'Why should they? They'll be Sydney people, mostly, I'll probably seem weird to them.'

'Of course you won't seem weird.'

Ruth had taken a cup from the draining board and dried it very carefully. 'What if I'm not as clever as you and the teachers think I am? What if I only *seem* clever, because I'm up here? And when I'm down in Sydney, where everyone else is clever, I'm just ordinary? Even stupid?'

'Ruth, don't be silly! Of course you're not stupid! What about your marks in the exams? Your scholarship? You beat a lot of Sydney people there.'

Ruth had put the cup carefully down on the table. 'Not stupid exactly,' she said, 'but—' She'd flung the tea towel aside and stood there in a sudden storm of tears. 'I don't want to go! I don't want to!'

'Oh, sweetheart!' Margaret May had put her arms round her and after a bit Ruth had stopped crying, and they'd gone on with the washing up and nothing else had been said. Last-minute nerves, that's all, Margaret May had told herself. It had to be – if Ruth didn't go it would be like – oh, it would be like those long-ago afternoons at the orphanage when, watching from a high window, Margaret May would see a car turn through the gates into the drive and really believe that it was someone kind come to take her away – and then it would only be the doctor, or one of the Sisters coming back from a visit, or someone to see Mother Evangeline.

BEHIND her in the kitchen they were still talking. 'And all that reading they had to do for their exams, poor loves,' Milly Lachlan was saying to Merle, as she wiped the drops of water from the big silver vase. 'All that studying. I know I'm an old softie but it seems wrong to me, somehow, when they're so young.'

'Well, it wouldn't do for me,' said Merle. 'Life! That's what you want! That's what you need to be good at, not books! What good did books ever do anyone?' She threw up her hands and waggled her fingers and shot a gleaming glance at Margaret May, who picked up a big silver vase of pink lilies and walked out of the kitchen, through the sacristy into the church, past the big statues with their staffs and shepherds crooks and crowns, past the long rows of polished pews, over to the little wooden Virgin standing patiently in her corner. 'There you are,' she said, placing the vase on the floor beside her, and then sitting down on the end of a pew to calm her angry feelings.

People like Merle had a down on reading, she thought. No, it was more than a down, it was stronger: it was suspicion and distrust, even a kind of jealousy, as if they thought there might be some secret dangerous treasure in those pages other people read that they themselves could never find. If the nuns at her old school caught you reading on the verandah at lunchtime, they made you get up and go out to play. There'd been no books at the orphanage except for holy ones, and as she got older Margaret May could see why: they were bringing you up to be a skivvy and reading might give you ideas.

'You don't get paid to *read*,' the housekeeper at *Fortuna* had said to her, snatching the old copy of *Romeo and Juliet* Margaret May had kept from school. She hadn't got it back until she'd left the place to marry Don Gower.

Don hadn't liked her reading either. In the first few months when he'd caught her browsing through a couple of tatty old books she'd picked up at the church fete, he'd only wrinkled his nose and asked her if she didn't have anything better to do. 'Isn't there some work you can get on with around the house?'

Later on, it got more serious. 'No reading when you're minding the shop,' he'd said. 'People'll come in and think you can't be bothered with 'em.'

He'd caught her twice. 'Haven't I told you about that?' The third time, an afternoon of heavy rain when no one would have come in anyway, his face had grown dark as the heavy sky outside.

She could see at once that he was in a mood. The way he went silent made you walk on tiptoe, and a panicky voice in your head kept crying silently, 'Talk to me! Talk!' He'd snatched the book and thrown it down. *Wuthering Heights*, it had been, and she'd thought how 'wuthering' was a good word for him, when he got a mood. 'I thought I told you,' he'd said, and he'd slapped her right across the face. 'There,' he'd said. 'Now *learn*.'

She hadn't learned. And neither would her Ruthie, if she had anything to do with it.

It had been another wuthering night when Don had died. He hadn't spoken to any of them for two whole weeks. It had been raining for days; their eldest, Charlie, had left his muddy gumboots in the hall and Don had tripped right over them. He'd punched Charlie in the mouth and a tooth had fallen out, a front tooth, a second tooth, lying there like a little white shell on the hall floor. Don had drawn his fist back for another go and Margaret May had grabbed his arm and then he'd hit her too and gone rushing out into the rain. She'd gone after him.

She wasn't having him punch the children in the face like that! No, she wasn't! She remembered the mud squelching under her feet as she followed him over the paddocks: his tall black shape at the edge of Skelly's dam, the glimmer of water – then he was gone.

She'd run for Father Joseph. There was a drowned calf in the water next to Don's body and Father Joseph and Doc O'Hare had told Sergeant Lawson that was how it had happened: Don had seen it struggling, tried to pull it out, then he'd slipped and fallen in. Sergeant Lawson had looked at Margaret May's bruised face but he hadn't asked her anything, not even why Don had been out walking in the rain.

Margaret May bowed her head into her hands. Oh, that her Ruth should ever have bruises on her face! And though she never said prayers, Margaret May couldn't stop herself from whispering, 'Please let her go to Sydney. Please let her go.'

'*Right* where people walk!' boomed a big voice in her ear, and she lifted her head and saw that Merle had followed her and was staring down at the vase of pink lilies.

'What did you say, Merle?'

'Right where people walk, that's what I said. *Right* where they'll kick it over.' She swooped down on the vase.

'Merle—' Milly Lachlan had come over. She touched Merle lightly on the arm.

Merle jerked round. 'What?' She clutched the vase of lilies to her chest, like a bridesmaid's pink bouquet.

'Leave it where it was,' said Milly. Her voice was gentle, but it held authority, and Merle spluttered like a defiant child. 'Why should I? It's dangerous, a big vase like that on a polished floor! I'm putting it next to the altar, where it's supposed to be, where decent people put it. These are *altar* vases.' She swept off down the aisle, leaving a trail of bright drops behind her.

'I'm sorry,' Milly said to Margaret May.

'It's not your fault.'

'No, but still, it's – upsetting.' Milly's voice warmed and she added, 'Margaret May, I'm so glad Ruth won her scholarship, I'm sure she'll do well at the university, and come to no harm at all in Sydney. Don't worry about what Father Joseph says, he's a bit old-fashioned, that's all. Ruth's a lovely girl.'

Margaret May's face lit with pleasure. 'And your Fee's lovely too; Ruth thinks the world of her, it's one of the things she's sad about, how she'll miss her very best friend.'

When Margaret May had gone home, Milly brought a cloth from the kitchen and wiped up the trail of drops that Merle had made.

Merle came and stood over her. 'I'm surprised that one can show her face in a church,' she said.

Milly looked up. 'Why shouldn't she?'

'Because she did it, you know.'

Milly frowned. 'Did what?'

'Pushed her hubby in the dam.'

Milly wrung the wet cloth into the bucket. She thought of that rainy night so long ago. She thought of that brute, Don Gower. She took the cloth out of the bucket and twisted it very hard. 'That's just an old tale, Merle,' she said. Though the trouble with old tales was that they stayed around, becoming truth to those who knew no better.

'And *she's* not so holy, either,' said Merle. 'She's up the spout and all!'

'What?'

'This one here.' Merle pointed to the little statue. She leaned down and patted the small bulge beneath the long plain shift. 'In the family way, see?'

'Well, what's wrong with that?' said Milly easily, and Merle, who'd wanted to make old Milly blush, was startled to find that her own large face had gone all hot and red and rude.

Twelve

Merle Hogan was halfway home down Starlight Lane when a wind got up, a cold wind funnelling up from out of the south. The grass in the paddocks thrilled and shuddered, bushes bowed over, branches lashed against the sky, and though the sun was still up there, high and bright, and a smell of smoke lingered from the grassfire over at Toysen's Flat, the air turned bitter cold. Crows called out like lost souls. 'Shut up,' Merle told them; she hated crows.

On her left the wind roared in the grove of she-oaks, to the right sun sparkled like ice on the surface of Skelly's dam. She stared across at the steep eroded banks and the dark water lapping far beneath them and muttered to herself, 'She did it all right, of course she did.' It gave you the creeps to think about: Margaret May sneaking after him across the paddocks in the dark and rain, her small face set with determination. Merle bet any money she wouldn't have turned a hair when he went in.

'Brrr,' she shivered, wondering whether anyone at home would have had the sense to get a fire going. Not Miss Helen, that was for sure. If she was cold, Helen would simply go to bed and pull the covers up and everyone else could go hang. She quickened her pace – Skelly's dam was a spooky place even in broad daylight, you'd never go there in the dark. There were stories that Don Gower's ghost roamed, the drowned calf tucked beneath his arm. Merle almost ran that last stretch down the lane and then galloped across the back paddock, the wind whipping at her hair.

THE minute she walked in the gate she knew there was something wrong. Len's ute was skewed sideways in front of the house, the driver's door hanging open. Merle's heart lurched: had something happened? One of the kids? She charged up the front steps, and as she reached the top the wire door crashed open and little Bridie came rushing out at her. 'Mum!' she yelled. 'Mum! Dad hit Helen! Dad hit Helen!'

'It's all right, love,' Merle gasped, 'it's all right. Mum's home now!' She gave the little girl a quick hug and burst into the house, straight through to the kitchen because that was where the trouble was, she could feel it, a kind of filthy shudder in the air. When she appeared in the doorway, the three of them went still as statues, little Petey saucer-eyed, squeezed in between the pantry and the stove, hiding; Len and Helen next to the window, hardly a foot of space between them, and on Helen's cheek the bright scarlet mark of a big broad hand.

He'd never hit her. Helen had always been his favourite one. Sometimes it seemed to Merle that everyone in the world was someone's favourite, except for her.

'What's happened? What's going on? Why'd you hit her?'

Len took a few steps towards her and threw out his hands. 'Bloody little – slut—' his voice almost broke on the word, 'won't tell me who he is!'

'Who? What? Speak plain!' But she knew. She'd had her suspicions for a while. Please God, let it be a *good* boy, she prayed silently, Let it be a *good* boy!

'That old fool Herb Tully—' Len began.

'Herb Tully!' The pinkness fled from Merle's wind-whipped face. The shock of Herb Tully made her body quiver all over, as if she'd had a blow. 'But—' she protested, barely able to take it in, 'but he's old enough to be her father!' She paused for a second, thinking about that, calculating, and then corrected, 'He's old enough to be her bloody *grandfather*!'

Len stared at his wife and slapped himself on the forehead in sheer amazement at what she'd said. 'Jesus, Merle! I didn't mean old Herb was up to anything with her! Of course I didn't!'

From the corner by the window came something between a sob and a giggle, a muffled snorting sound. Len threw a furious glance towards it, and bawled out, 'And you can just shut up over there, unless you want to feel the back of my hand again!' His eyes had gone all small and red, Merle noticed, like when he had a cold.

'So what's old Herb Tully got to do with it, then?' she prompted.

'Herb Tully come up to me outside the pub, didn't he? Told me he was takin' a stroll through Perry's orchard on Wednesday night and he saw—' Len jerked his head wordlessly in Helen's direction, as if he couldn't bear to speak her name, 'that one with some boy.' He spat suddenly and shockingly down onto her best lino. '*Under* some boy, that'd be.'

Merle ignored the spitting. 'What business was it of Herb Tully's, I'd like to know!' she shrieked, venting her anger on the messenger. 'He's a bloody old woman!'

'Yeah, love, I know he is. I told him so.'

He had, too, more or less. 'What business is it of yours?' he'd demanded, and Herb had replied nervously, twirling his old hat in his hands, 'Thought you'd want to know, Len. Before anything came of it, like, before—'

Len had cut him short. 'Who's the boy?'

Herb's watery blue eyes had flickered. 'I couldn't say. It was dark under all them trees, and he was – I couldn't see his face.'

'How come you knew it was my girl then?'

And then Herb had grinned – a weak, knowing grin that Len had wanted to wipe right off his face. 'It was that red dress of hers,' smirked Herb. 'I'd know it anywhere!'

'Would ya, ya mongrel!' Len had shouted, and Herb had scuttled back a few steps.

'Easy on, mate! How'd it get to be my fault?'

'Ah, get out!' Pushing Herb Tully aside, Len had rushed to his ute, jumped in and sped away. Now, in the privacy of his own kitchen, he roared, 'Bloody red dress! Look at it, willya? Makes her look like a tart! Makes her look like she's up for anything! And she probably got it too!'

'Len!' But she saw where he was pointing: the big rip in Helen's dress. It was right up the front, the skirt nearly torn in two – Merle almost flew to the spot where Helen lounged against the window. She grabbed her by the arm.

'Ow! Let go!'

'Who's the boy?'

'Ow! You're pinching me!' Helen pulled away.

'Who's the boy, I said!'

'I been asking her that!' cried Len. 'Waddya think I've been doin' for the last bloody hour? She won't say anything!' His big chin wobbled, like he was going to cry. 'But she's goin' to—' He strode across to Helen and raised his hand.

Merle pounced and grabbed it. 'No more of that! Helen, who is it, now?'

Helen stared out the window.

'I'm gonna knock her for six if she doesn't tell,' promised Len. 'I am, God help me!'

Over on the mantel, the wireless had been playing soft music all this time. Now the six o'clock pips sounded, and the Angelus began. *Hail Mary, full of grace, the Lord is with thee; blessed art thou among women and blessed is the fruit of thy womb, Jesus.*

The two adults cringed on the word 'womb'. The girl tossed her head. The funny thing was how they all said 'Amen' at the end, even Petey in his hidey-hole and little Bridie outside in the hall. Then it was back to business.

'Who is he, Hellie?' growled Merle through clenched teeth.

Still she wouldn't say. Only then Petey shrieked out, 'It's Tam Finn! Hellie's in love with Tam Finn!'

Merle's heart dropped right down. Mother of God! Of all the boys in Barinjii, she had to go and pick *that* one!

Len roared, '*That* crazy bugger!'

They looked at each other. They both knew that if anything came of it, the Finns wouldn't want to hear.

'Jesus wept!' moaned Len.

'Hellie's in love with Tam Finn!' shrieked Petey again, and Helen rushed from the window, dragged him from his hiding place and whacked him over the head. Merle surged after her and slapped the unmarked cheek. 'Now you've got a pair!' she shrilled. 'And just you remember this, my girl: if you're up the spout, I'm not havin' you in the house! And you needn't think you're goin' to Sydney to get rid of it, either! It'll be the nuns for you!'

Helen rushed out into the hall, stumbling over little Bridie who'd been sitting just outside the door, a Little Golden Book held up to cover her face. Helen grabbed *The Pokey Little Puppy* and hurled it against the wall. Then she ran down the hall to her room and Bridie ran after her, sobbing.

'Get out!' yelled Helen, and slammed the door. She flung herself down on the bed. She hated Dad! And Mum as well! They could bloody mind their own business! It was *her* life, wasn't it? She scrubbed at her eyes, she sniffed and rubbed her nose. Then she jumped up again and looked down at herself. She looked at the big rip in her dress – he'd done that on purpose, Tam Finn! She hated him, too!

No, she didn't.

Suddenly she didn't want to be in the room anymore. She ran to the window, pushed it up and jumped out into the windswept afternoon. She ran round the side and up past the sheds to where the old windmill creaked upon its rusty frame.

'You kids keep away from that thing,' Dad had warned them, 'it's gonna go one day!'

'Too bad,' muttered Helen, climbing up onto the crossbar, high as she could go, straddling it, legs dangling, wind rushing all round her. Too bad if she fell! Too bad if she got killed! They'd be sorry then! They'd blub in church and out in the graveyard, all right, Mum and Dad and the littlies! Blub and blub and blub! And Tam Finn – Helen went still, thinking what Tam Finn would do when he heard she'd died. Nothing, she decided. Nothing's what he'd do. And he'd feel nothing. He was like that. One day, she thought, he'd marry a girl from a rich family who'd been to some posh private school and didn't know a thing. They'd live out at *Fortuna* and have proper little kids – and Tam Finn would feel nothing for them, nothing at all. 'So, yah! rich girl from a private school!' cried Helen, 'See how you like *that*!' And she stuck her tongue out as far as it would go.

The wind dropped suddenly. The air went still. Helen gathered her skirt up and examined the tear. It was a straight rip down the seam; Mum would probably be able to mend it for her, when she got in a better mood. Though that might take a while. Helen sniffed again, pushed her hair behind her ears, and looked out over the land. You got a great view from up here, you could see the whole world – their world, that was: past Skelly's dam and Starlight Lane, over the paddocks to the green line of the creek, the little farms with their sheds and barns, and far away a great swathe of deeper green that was the beginning of the *Fortuna* property, its gardens and lawns and big old trees. Helen turned her head away from it;

she knew she'd never get to go there, never get to see the peacock, whose name Tam wouldn't tell her, or the famous lake where water lilies bloomed.

Closer in was the town itself: Main Street with its shops and houses, the streets and lanes behind it, the school and the churches and the silos out by the railway line. She saw no sign of Tam Finn, but down in Main Street a small figure in a prissy blue skirt was hurrying past the post office towards Gower's Store.

Ruth Gower. Little Miss High-and-Mighty-Teacher's-Pet, another one who didn't know a thing. She'd get what was coming to her one day all right! Helen stuck her tongue out again. And yah! to *her*, as well.

IN the living room of the house on Hopeton Street, Milly Lachlan was giving her granddaughter another fitting for the wedding dress. The bodice was too tight, Fee said – and round the waist as well.

'Keep still now,' Milly told her through a mouthful of pins. 'Just this last little bit here—'

'Ruth's going tomorrow night!' said Fee. 'She's really, *really* going!' She shook her fair curls dazedly.

'Keep still, lovie.'

'But I can hardly believe it's true! Imagine Ruth not being here!'

'Ah well,' sighed Milly. 'These things happen; people grow up and go to other places.'

'But she's my *best friend*!'

'Even best friends. She'll come back on visits.'

'But not for *good*.'

'Ah well,' sighed Milly again.

'I'd be scared if it was me,' confided Fee.

'Would you, lovie?'

'I like it here,' said Fee.

Milly smiled and pinned in the very last tuck. 'There!' she said. 'You can look in the mirror now.'

Fee picked up her satin skirts and skipped across the room. 'Oh!' she breathed. 'Oh! It's beautiful! I can't believe it's really me!'

'It's you, all right,' said Milly.

The beautiful dress fell round Fee's young body like a river of soft light. 'Mattie won't know me,' she said.

'Oh, he will,' said Milly, 'if he's got eyes to see.'

'He's got eyes,' smiled Fee. 'My lovely Mattie.' And she ran a hand down the wedding dress, across her breast, down past her waist, which wasn't as narrow as it used to be, lingering gently on the new special place beneath the shining satin. She looked up and caught her grandmother's smiling eyes. They grinned at each other.

From the kitchen came the rattle of dishes and the murmur of placid conversation. Fee's mum and dad were in there washing the dishes together, like they did every night. Mrs Lachlan washed, and Mr Lachlan dried.

Fee stroked her tummy dreamily. 'Don't tell them, all right?' she whispered to her gran. 'We're going to say it's premature.'

'As if I'd tell,' said Milly.

FATHER Joseph was out watering his tomatoes. The sun was setting, a great ball of crimson fire over the western plains. There'd been a grassfire over at Toysen's Flat this afternoon, and the smell of smoke still drifted, mingling with the scent of water on damp green leaves. '*Glory be to God in Heaven, Peace to those who love him well,*' carolled Father Joseph, and then, pausing to adjust the nozzle on his hose, he heard a faint echo of his Gloria drifting back from the paddocks beyond the fence. The sound went on and on – not an echo then, but someone out there, whistling his hymn. Father Joseph put the hose down and went to the back gate. A lonely figure was walking along the track towards him. A man, he thought at first, but as the whistler came closer, the slightness of his figure, and something in the way he moved, something at once fluid and uncertain, made him realise it was a boy. And then the whistling became a voice whose melancholy sweetness made the old man's hand go to his heart.

Glory be to God in Heaven, Peace to those who love him well—

Father Joseph thought an angel might sing like that.

The boy was close now, still swinging along the track, only a little way off across the tussocky grass, passing parallel to Father Joseph's back gate. The last of the light showed a pale narrow face, the shine of blue-black hair – 'Tam!' called Father Joseph, because yes, it was the Finn boy. 'Tam Finn!'

The boy stopped singing and stood still.

'Tam Finn!' the old priest called again, but the boy made no reply.

They were strange, the Finns. He thought of the time last

Christmas when Harry Finn and his old mother had come to Mass. 'How's the boy?' Father Joseph had asked them. 'How's Tam?'

'He's fine,' Harry Finn had replied, and then old Mrs Finn had recited, in her clipped fluting voice, 'Tam is Tam and all alone, and evermore shall be so.'

Daft as a brush, Father Joseph had thought.

'Tam! It's me, boy! Father Joseph! Over here!'

This time the boy turned his head. In the fading light his eyes looked like two wicked fingermarks on the immaculate pallor of his face. He said nothing, but from his lips there came a low, savage hiss. Father Joseph felt the hate of it like a burn in his gut; he stepped back and crossed himself. The boy ran on along the track and the strange fluidity of his movements reminded the old man suddenly of a whirlwind he'd seen once, out Wilcannia way.

And yet, as he turned in to his house, Father Joseph had the strangest feeling. It was almost a kind of guilt about the boy, as if there was something he'd missed, and kept on missing. Something he should have *seen,* he thought, blundering along the dark hall towards his study.

But what? He had no idea. 'Ah, Mammy,' he whispered, 'it's a useless old thing I am these days.' He entered the stuffy little room and reached for the light, and then stood a long while gazing round him at the clutter and a big moth dancing round the lamp, and the chair that his Maidie had sat in when she'd quarrelled with him, three weeks and two whole days ago.

Thirteen

Ruth was packing the small suitcase that she would carry with her on the train. This time tomorrow night she'd be on the 7.20 down. She folded her new nightie and summer dressing gown, her new underwear, the clothes for her very first day in Sydney. She was placing them in layers, carefully, the nightie on the top, all ready, when all at once she stopped and sat down on the bed to cry. Which was stupid, of course, but it was all the last things, all this week, so many last things: the last time she'd catch the bus with Nan to go shopping in Dubbo; the last time she and Fee would spend a lazy Saturday afternoon together, doing nothing in particular, sitting talking on the verandah, kicking their feet in the ferns; the last time she'd walk over the paddocks to Benson's farm to get a pot of Dad's favourite honey for their tea.

'They're *not* last times,' Nan had insisted this morning. 'You'll be back for Fee's wedding, and for the holidays—'

Oh, she was sick of hearing that, sick of it! And whatever people said, it *wouldn't* be the same. She got up from the bed and stood staring down at the open suitcase, the neat folded clothes, and she felt in her heart that she honestly didn't want to go away. She wouldn't mind going to the teachers' college, or even working in a bank – oh no, *she* wouldn't mind. It was Nan who would hate it. Ruth picked up the new nightie and flung it on the floor. It was Nan who would hate the teachers' college instead of university, who would hate Dubbo instead of Sydney – it was Nan who wanted her to have this new life! And Nan wanted it for *herself*, not for Ruth, not really. She wanted it to make up for all the bad things in her own life: for the orphanage, and being a servant out at *Fortuna*, and the husband she never spoke about, who people said she'd pushed into the dam. She wanted Ruth to live the life she'd never had, the life where you might find the real true thing.

But Ruth didn't want to live someone else's dreams. She wanted her own. And she wanted all the old familiar things: this room with its shabby furniture, this house, the verandah where she sat on summer evenings, Nan's beautiful garden. She didn't want to be a stranger in a huge unknown city. She wanted to be in Barinjii, walking down the main street where she knew the names of every person going by, every dog stretched out on the warm footpath, every cat on a window-sill – and where, at any moment, she might turn a corner and see Tam Finn.

And Nan was making her leave. 'I won't,' said Ruth, 'I won't and she can't make me! And I'm going to tell her now!' She slammed down the lid of the suitcase and hurried from the room, pausing on the landing for a moment, peering down into the hallway where, less than a month ago, she'd looked down and seen the letter from the university lying beneath the door. That day seemed like years ago. She was a different person now.

Down there the hallway was in darkness except for a narrow strip of light gleaming from beneath the closed door of the living room. Dad had gone to bed an hour back; she'd heard his faint shuffly footsteps coming up the stairs, and that small soft sigh he always gave as he opened the door of his room. But Nan was still up. Nan was in that lighted room. In a moment, Ruth would go down there. *'It's you!'* she'd say to her, flinging open the door. 'It's *you* who wants to go, not me! It's *you* who wants to have that wonderful new life!' And then – and then Nan would turn round and look at her and there'd be that orphanage expression in her eyes, only this time Ruth would take no notice of it, she wouldn't give in. Not this time! she vowed, running down the stairs, crossing the hall, standing still outside the closed door.

There was no sound from inside the living room, not the faintest murmur, no click of knitting needles or the soft turning of a page. She reached for the doorknob, it felt smooth and cold in her hand. She turned it slowly, already uncertainty was creeping over her, and she opened the door so quietly her nan didn't even hear her come in.

Margaret May was sitting at the table reading in the way she always did: her eyes moving rapidly along the lines, her thumb and finger poised ready to turn the next page and the next, quickly, quickly, quickly! as if she feared that at any moment someone might come and snatch the book away.

'Nan?'

Nan looked up. The expression on her face was one that Ruth had never seen there before but which she recognised right away. It was panic. It was as if Nan had guessed everything that Ruth had been thinking upstairs in her room, knew every single word her granddaughter had planned to say, and now she sat waiting for the expected blow to fall, as she must have waited many times before when bad things had happened.

'Ruthie,' she said in a low flat voice. 'Is something wrong?' Her eyes looked blind.

'No,' said Ruth helplessly. She couldn't say those things she'd planned. She wasn't that kind of person. She'd be going down to Sydney after all. 'Nothing's wrong, Nan,' she said. 'I just came to say goodnight again, since it's my very last night here.' Her bare feet trod heavily across the carpet, she stooped and kissed the dry cheek, imagining she tasted a kind of terror there. 'Goodnight again,' she said softly.

Margaret May took Ruth's hand and held it tenderly. 'Thank you, my Ruthie,' she said, 'thank you.'

Ruth went upstairs. She picked the new nightdress up from the floor, folded it neatly and placed it back inside the suitcase, all ready for tomorrow night, all ready for the 7.20 down. She finished the rest of her packing, turned out the light and went to bed. A few minutes later she heard Nan come upstairs and walk softly down the passage to her room. Her door closed. Ruth fell asleep and woke again, suddenly, her mind filled with the image of Helen Hogan down by the creek, her red dress, the blood, her mocking voice saying, 'Just remember that you know nothing, okay?'

A gust of warm wind blew through the curtains and rattled at the blind, and the scents of smoke and dust and baked grasses filled the shadowy room. In Sydney there'd be different scents: the smells of streets and crowds and petrol and the sea. She got up and went to the window, staring out at the familiar buildings across the road: the dark closed fronts of the bank and the community hall, the bakery and Mr Tanner's butcher's shop, the post office where a single light was burning in an upstairs room, as if old Joanie Fawkes also found it difficult to get to sleep.

A night bird called out across the paddocks – what if she never found anyone to love her down in Sydney?

Somewhere in the street a door slammed, Bang! Then there was silence, into which the old hymn came drifting, faintly at first, so she couldn't be quite sure she wasn't imagining it, and then clearer and clearer, like a shadow that close up reveals itself to be a man.

Come down, O love divine,
Seek now this heart of mine—

He was singing the words this time, and out there in the night the hymn sounded purer, more lovely than it had ever sounded in Father Joseph's church on Sundays, as if each word was rimmed with the most tender love.

Tam Finn was out there. Excitement welled in her; she didn't hesitate. Pulling on her skirt and blouse, pushing her feet into sandals, she hardly noticed what she was doing, she was breathless, desperate to get outside before Tam Finn disappeared. When she rushed through the front door, the street was empty but the hymn drifted down it, riding in from the paddocks on that warm scented wind. She ran towards it, past the shops and houses and on into the paddocks where the moon seemed brighter, a big half moon like a bowl of shining blessings tipped over the land. As she turned into Starlight Lane Tam Finn stepped out of the grove of she-oaks, exactly as he'd done that first time. 'Ruth,' he said softly. 'Here's Ruthie.'

She stood still, her breath so quick and loud she seemed to be almost panting, like Fee's old dog Rusty, when he stood in the kitchen waiting while Mrs Lachlan cut up his meat. It was a wanting sort of sound, and she hated it, she couldn't bear that it should come from her mouth. The excitement dropped from her and she looked around, hardly able to believe she'd come here, blindly, like the sleepwalker in Helen Hogan's old story, as if another person lived inside her and did these things, a person who felt, who wanted, who went ahead without a word. One minute you were leaning on the windowsill of your old room, and the next – she turned to go back but Tam Finn reached out and placed his hands on her shoulders. 'So you came,' he said. 'You know, I thought you might.'

She looked up at him. His face was thinner and the skin around his eyes had a blueish tinge, as if he'd been ill. But perhaps it was only the moonlight, shining down on him.

'So-o,' he murmured, smiling. 'What do you want, little Ruthie?'

She looked away from him, down at her feet. Moonlight glittered on the buckles of her sandals and seemed to wink at her.

'Here's a girl who doesn't know what she wants!' said Tam Finn, and then his arms went round her and his body was all bones and sharp nagging angles and there was no comfort in it and nothing you could imagine to be love, even when he lowered his head and she felt his lips move gently against her hair. 'She doesn't know at all,' whispered Tam Finn. 'But I do, I know what this girl wants.'

A light flashed suddenly behind them and Ruth jerked her head sideways to see. The porch light had come on in the Hogans' house on top of the hill.

'They can't see us,' said Tam Finn. 'Not from up there on the hill. Not when we're in the dark down here.'

A small child's voice cried out, ''Bonny! Here, Bonny, Bonny, Bonny! Good girl, Bonny!' The light went out. A door slammed. Silence fell again.

Tam Finn laughed softly. 'Good girl, Ruthie,' he said, catching her chin in his long fingers, raising her face to him. 'Oh, good girl!' His grip on her body tightened, she closed her eyes and his mouth came down on hers; she felt the wetness of his lips, his tongue, and the utter strangeness of another person's breathing turning into hers. She opened her eyes and saw his eyes, their dark rainy grey and a cloudiness beneath it like the sediment of poison at the bottom of a cup. The sediment shifted, and once again she had the impression of that other person hiding there, that frightened, importunate stranger knocking at her door.

He drew his mouth from hers and pressed her face down against his chest. 'Let me, ah, let me,' he whispered hoarsely, and for a moment she thought perhaps he was saying, 'help me,' but all around them the trees were whispering and stirring, and the sound of her blood was rushing in her ears and she couldn't be sure. His hand slipped beneath her skirt and there was the sudden shock of cold metal, of the snake ring against the warm flesh of her thigh. Over his shoulder she saw a strange moving glimmer on the hillside; the wind and moonlight had caught the dark water of the dam and it gleamed down at them. The sight made her gasp and pull away from him, and Tam Finn didn't try to stop her.

'Ah well,' he said sadly, and he leaned his face against her breast for the briefest of moments, before turning to see where she was staring. 'The dam,' he said, 'where they say your nan pushed your grandpa in.'

'She didn't.'

'You're right,' he said, smiling his lovely smile. 'She didn't, Ruthie; that's only a Barinjii tale. They're fond of tales round here.'

'I know.'

'Your nan wouldn't hurt a fly.'

'I know,' she said again, eagerly.

He nodded. 'Good,' and then he added, 'She gave me something once.'

'Gave you something? Nan?'

'She gave me a smile, right in the middle of Main Street. It mightn't sound like anything much, but I loved it. Not so many people smile at me round here, you know. She was kind.'

She looked up at his face. She thought, he sees people, how they are. She thought he might even be good, in a way that most people never were. 'Tam,' she said, and knew with a shocking certainty that it was the only time she'd ever say his name to him.

He touched two fingers against his lips and pressed them against her forehead. 'Well, little schoolteacher,' he said, 'off you go then.'

'But—' she hesitated, and he touched her gently on the shoulder.

'Go on down to Sydney, Ruthie. It's right for you.'

'Is it?'

'It's your place. You're lucky to have a place. I wish I had.'

She stared at him. 'But – but you've got *Fortuna*!'

'Oh, *Fortuna*.' He looked away. 'Perhaps.'

'But—'

'Off you go, Ruthie. You go home now, before I change my mind.'

'But you—'

'Don't worry about me. There's plenty more fish in the sea, eh? Plenty more little fishies.' He shoved his hands into his pockets and began to walk away down Starlight Lane, whistling his old hymn again. In the bright moonlight, before he passed into the shadows of the trees, she saw the brave tilt of his head, the narrowness of his shoulders and the way he held them, straight and defiant, like a little kid, like someone very young who was saying with his body, which was all he had, 'I don't care.'

It made her want to cry, it made her want to run after him. She didn't; she turned the other way and began to walk slowly back towards the town.

THAT night Father Joseph had a dream of cloven hooves and shaggy muscled legs and little Ruth Gower's sweet white body held fast between them, her small breasts grasped in brutal, hairy hands.

He woke and sat up in bed. His skin was clammy and sweat dripped from his forehead. It was dread, he thought, dread of what would become of Maidie's girl down there in that sink of iniquity. He was old, he knew – his congregation was dwindling, the young ones were drifting away, the pew beside the confessional was empty most Saturdays – but while he had breath in him, that girl would be saved. He would shame Margaret May into keeping young Ruth in Barinjii. He would force Maidie's hand.

Father Joseph switched on the light and opened the drawer of his bedside table. He'd already written his sermon for tomorrow, but he knew now it wouldn't do. He took out the pad of paper, ripped out the sheets, and started all over again.

fourteen

It was Sunday morning. Margaret May was halfway to Saint Columba's when Ruth came running after her. 'I'm coming with you,' she said.

'To church? I thought you said you weren't going anymore.'

'I'm not,' said Ruth. 'Just this very last time, with you.' She took Margaret May's hand, and together they walked on up the hill.

'Nan?'

'Yes?'

'Nan, I *really* want to go to Sydney now. I didn't, before.'

'You had me worried there for a little while,' said Nan. Today her voice sounded so light and carefree that it was hard to believe in the panic Ruth had seen last night.

'Did I? I think I was afraid, a bit,' said Ruth. 'I wasn't *sure*.'

'And now you are?'

'Yes.'

'Has something happened?' asked Margaret May, with a quick sideways glance into the girl's bright face. 'To make you change your mind?'

'No, no, nothing,' replied Ruth quickly, pushing the memories of last night away, the roughness of Tam Finn's shirt against her cheek, the warmth of him, his thin black shadow vanishing down the lane – and pushing away the strange feeling of failure that had crept over her later when she was lying alone in her room. 'I've been thinking, Nan, that's all. I think Sydney's *my place*.' Her brown eyes fixed intently on her grandmother's face. 'My *place*. You know?'

'I think I do,' said Margaret May.

THEY sat close together, three rows from the front of the church, in the seat that was nearest the little statue. The vase of pink lilies had gone; Merle Hogan had taken them away.

After the readings, Father Joseph unfurled the newspaper he'd carried with him up the steps of the pulpit and held it out dramatically towards the congregation. There was a startled intake of breath, for the newspaper was *The Record*, a publication against which he railed so often that many of them bought it to see what the old man was on about, and found it a good Sunday read. Even those in the middle rows today could make out the banner headlines screaming from the front page: *Sex Scandals Rock Our Universities!* Father Joseph turned a page to a double spread of photographs: fine old stone buildings set amongst heavy-leaved English trees.

Ruth didn't notice; she was thinking of Tam Finn. She wondered what he was doing now; she wondered if he knew she was going tonight. She thought of his voice urging her,

'Let me, oh, let me!' She should have let him, she should have! Only – what would have happened then? Afterwards? She frowned, remembering Helen Hogan down at the creek in her torn dress, and Meg Harrison bawling in the washroom, and girls like Kathy Ryan who'd had to go away. Perhaps it would have been different for her. Would it have been?

'Sex Scandals Rock Our University!' Father Joseph roared, and Ruth's head jerked up – all round her the congregation was rippling like long grass in the wind and heads were turning towards the place where she and Nan were sitting. Everyone knew Ruth Gower was going off to Sydney University, that she was booked on the evening train, that already her luggage had been delivered to the stationmaster's office and was waiting for the 7.20 down.

'University, they call it!' Father Joseph jeered. 'The seat of learning! The ivory towers!' Spit flew from his mouth; he wiped his lips with the back of his hand. 'You know what I call it? I call it the *Sink*. Yes, you heard me! Not Mum's kitchen sink where you all go to wash your hands at teatime, but the Sink of Iniquity!'

Margaret May leaned towards Ruth and whispered, 'Do you want to go home, sweetheart?'

'No,' said Ruth. 'I'm staying here with you!'

Down at the back, Merle Hogan was craning forward to see the pair of them. She noticed how Margaret May was sitting with her back poker straight: a habit she'd have learned at the orphanage. The girl was white as a sheet hung out to dry.

Father Joseph rose on the balls of his feet. 'They teach Free Love down there!' he bellowed, shaking his fist in the air.

Merle nudged her husband's Sunday jacket. 'He's on a roll!'

'Teachers, they call themselves? *I* say beguilers! Beguilers who would sully the purity of the young!' His gaze swept down on Ruth; she stared back at him defiantly. He paused and then said almost casually, 'The Abortion Car.'

There was another gasp, and from somewhere in the middle of the congregation, a small muffled scream.

'Oh yes, you've heard of it, I see! That big black car that leaves the doctors' surgeries of our big city on Mondays and Thursdays, carrying its freight to butchery and Hell! And who are these poor damned souls who ride in it? Who?' He leaned over the edge of the pulpit and the congregation held their breath. The silence was so complete that you could hear, from that other church way down the bottom of the hill, a hymn flowing out into the innocent morning air:

All things bright and beautiful,
all creatures great and small,
all things wise and wonderful,
The Lord God made them all.

Someone hastened to close the door.

'And who *are* those poor girls?' repeated Father Joseph.

Now the silence bristled with anticipation and something which was almost like greed: Ruth could feel the eyes hovering at her back like blowflies feasting on infection.

'*I'll* tell you who they are!' roared the priest. 'They're bright girls, girls with ambition, girls who imagined, who were *told*, that the university would give them a chance for a better life!' He banged his fist on the pulpit's rim. 'Though what better life can there be for a young woman than to be the centre of her own home and family? What better life?' His fist thumped relentlessly, again and again, so that the small church resounded with its violence and a child cried out, 'I want to go ho-ome!'

He paused while the child was carried outside and the doors closed once more, then the fist banged down again. 'And who is to blame?'

Heads that had turned to watch the child being carried out of church now swivelled back to Margaret May. They all knew how the old woman had defied him; the tale was all around the town. Their eyes drove in, examining Margaret May minutely: the way she sat, the expression on her face, her hat, her dress – and every little thing seemed wrong. The colour of her lipstick was too bright, surely, for a woman of her age.

'Who then is to blame?' Father Joseph asked them again, and another child called out, 'The Devil!'

'The Devil, yes,' the old man agreed. 'The Devil entering into a heart!' He looked down at the place where Margaret May was sitting and caught her fierce bright eyes. He trembled. The *look* she gave him, piercing as an angel's sword – it brought the memories crowding: the first time he'd seen her, the tiny solid weight of the baby the nurse had put into his arms, the great glowing eyes of the little creature turned up to his face! The young Margaret May climbing down from the sulky on that morning he'd driven her to *Fortuna*; catching her stocking on a rough piece of wood, tearing a big jagged hole and crying out, 'Oh! The nuns'll kill me!' And him saying, 'Those nuns are back where we left 'em, Maidie, far, far away!' And the smile she'd given him! Like the sun in all its splendour! The old man swallowed, and for a moment his resolve faltered, but then he thought of the girl and the fate that would surely be hers down in Sydney, and so he took a quick breath and went on again.

'What would you say to a mother, a grandmother! who allowed – no! encouraged! the young girl left in her care to go down to this Sodom, this Gomorrah?'

'Aa-aah!' the congregation breathed. They shook their heads, and drew their lips in tight and frowned seriously at each other.

The priest raised a hand and scratched at the rim of his left ear. Merle nudged Len excitedly. 'Vinny Gower used to do that, remember? Scratch his ear like that, in school, when the teachers asked him a question?'

'Shh,' Len urged her, for in her excitement Merle was speaking quite loudly.

'*I* say that such a woman has betrayed God's sacred trust,' Father Joseph pronounced. '*I* say she has endangered her soul and the soul placed in her care! *I* say that such a woman has committed a kind of – a kind of *murder*—'

The moment the word was out of his mouth a forest of whispers sprang up: everyone knew the old rumours about Don Gower's drowning: how some people said Margaret May had pushed him in the dam and others said Father Joseph had helped her and still more believed the bloke had fallen in himself, dragging out a calf—

The church buzzed.

Up there above them Father Joseph had fallen silent, and an expression of dull shock was gathering on his heavy features. Murder! Why had he gone and said that word? He hadn't meant to. He knew the rumours, of course, and to tell the truth he'd never been entirely sure himself, there'd been those bruises, and Maidie had never come to confession since that night. For weeks after the drowning he'd lain awake at night, tossing and turning, staring into the dark.

But still, he hadn't meant to say the word murder. Writing the sermon last night he'd used a different one – what had it been now? Father Joseph pulled at his ear. What had it been? He couldn't remember, and now his eyes had gone foggy, the faces of the congregation blurred before him. For a second he thought he saw his mother standing by the door, in her blue dress and old cracked boots, one hand up to her hair. Then she was gone again.

What was the word? The one he'd used instead of murder?

Then he had it. Destruction, that was it. 'A kind of destruction' – that's what he'd meant to say. 'A kind of destruction,' he said aloud into the whispering, 'not – not a kind of murder.'

They didn't seem to hear him.

'In the name of the Father, and the Son, and the Holy Ghost,' he said quickly, and made the sign of the cross over them all.

Margaret May sat unmoving, while the mass continued and communicants passing up the aisle sneaked quick sidelong glances in her direction. The night that Don had died was coming back to her again: the cold and the rain, the black water of the dam: how Don had gone down and then come up and then gone down again and how then there'd been nothing, an utter silence, except for the pattering of the rain. 'They'll never believe me,' she'd sobbed at the presbytery door. 'They'll say I pushed him in.'

Then there'd been the warmth of his big solid arm around her cold shoulders, and his strong voice saying, 'They'll believe *me*, Maidie.'

She would never speak to him again, vowed Margaret May now. She would never come back to this place.

The church was empty. Ruth was pulling at her sleeve. 'Are you all right, Nan?' she was saying.

'Yes,' she answered, keeping her voice steady. 'Are you?'

Ruth nodded. 'Course I am. But—' She frowned, studying Margaret May's pale face. 'I can still go, can't I, Nan? Down to Sydney? You aren't going to listen to *him*?'

'Of course I'm not.' Margaret May's voice grew hard. 'There's no way I'd stop you doing anything on that old fool's say-so.'

'Though he's your friend,' Ruth said uneasily.

'Was,' said Margaret May. 'Was my friend.'

There was a little silence. Margaret May looked up at the vaulted ceiling, and then at the radiant windows, at the grace-ful stone font, the statues of Saint Michael with his great wings and shining sword and Christ with his arms outspread – and last of all at the little Virgin in her corner. The Virgin's face was unperturbable as always. Here I stand, that calm face seemed to say, here I stand, and they rain down on me: prayers for the sick and dying; prayers for the dead and grieving, for the poor and the weak, the wicked, the lost and the mad. Here I stand and their rain falls down on me and still I go on staying.

Ruth glanced out through the open door at the little groups of people buzzing on the lawn. 'No one'll talk to you now, Nan,' she whispered.

'Oh, they will, they will,' replied Margaret May. 'Eventually. The talk'll die down, like it did before, when something else comes along for them to wag their tongues about.' She patted Ruth's hand. 'And there's always good people, Ruthie, don't forget that. Even in a little place like Barinjii – people with kindness, people with good sense, people they can't fool.' Margaret May thought of little Milly Lachlan and smiled.

She got to her feet and tucked the girl's arm in hers. 'Come on, let's go.'

fifteen

'I wish your dad could have come with us to the station,' sighed Fee, 'to see you off on the train.'

'Well, you know how he is,' said Ruth. 'Ever since the accident he's been afraid to go in a car. And we said goodbye at home.'

Fee squeezed her hand. They were standing on the platform, waiting for the 7.20 down. Fee looked up towards the stationmaster's office where Margaret May had gone to check that Ruth's big luggage was ready for the train. 'Mattie and me, we want you to know we'll keep an eye on your nan while you're away, okay? Me and Mattie and Mum and Dad and Mattie's mum and dad. And Grandma too – Grandma Milly, she loves your nan.'

'Thank you,' whispered Ruth, and her eyes filled with tears, and then Fee's eyes began to fill with tears, and 'Yeah, well,' said Mattie, 'I think I'll just go and sit in the car for a bit, leave you two girls to say goodbye and stuff—'

'Mattie! You're not going anywhere! And haven't you forgotten something?'

'What?'

Fee rolled her eyes at him.

'Oh yeah.' Mattie turned towards Ruth. He stood awkwardly before her like a shy boy with a bunch of flowers for the teacher. He cleared his throat. 'Ruth! I just want to wish you all the best in Sydney! Hope it's good down there and—' He was blushing now, a fierce red blush, all the way up his neck to his chin and cheeks and broad forehead and into his straw-coloured hair.

'Oh Mattie, thank you!' said Ruth, and he leaned closer and planted a kiss on her cheek. 'Hope all your dreams come true,' he mumbled, and then Fee cried out excitedly, 'Here's your nan! And look! The train's coming!'

Further up the platform Fred Wheeler had emerged from his office and Margaret May was hurrying towards them. Behind her, still a long way off, they could see a tiny black engine trailing a short row of dusty wooden carriages down the single narrow track.

'It doesn't look big enough to take you all those miles and miles away,' said Fee, holding tight to Ruth's hand. But close up the train seemed huge, the black sides of the engine sheer as cliffs of shining coal.

'It's a little early,' Margaret May told them. 'Fred says we've got five more minutes to say our goodbyes.'

'Right!' Mattie grabbed Ruth's small suitcase. 'I'll put your bag in your compartment then. Car D, isn't it?'

Ruth nodded. 'Compartment seven.'

Fee ran after him. 'I'm coming too!'

Margaret May and Ruth were left alone.

Ruth couldn't look at the train that stood waiting, or even

at her nan. Instead, she stared out beyond the station at the way they'd come, where the late sun lay heavy and gold on the paddocks and you could see the cluster of roofs and treetops that was Barinjii, far off at the end of the road.

Margaret May took both Ruth's hands in hers. 'Well,' she said. 'Well, Ruthie, here you go.'

Ruth's throat felt swollen, almost closed. 'Oh, Nan,' she said at last, swallowing hard and then leaning forward to kiss the old lady's cheek, and Margaret May brushed the damp hair from the girl's forehead, smoothing it gently back over the crown of her head, in long strokes, like a blessing, over and over and over. 'Be happy,' she said softly. 'Be happy, Ruthie.'

Ruth nodded dumbly. 'I'll try,' was all she could find to say.

Fee and Mattie came hurtling from the train. 'Oh, it's so lovely, your cabin!' cried Fee. 'It's got a little sink, with a tiny cake of soap, like you'd find in a doll's house – and cupboards, and a seat that turns into a bed, with sheets and a blanket and pillows—' She was laughing with delight, and all three of them smiled and gazed at her with love, and Ruth thought how Fee was the kind of person you just hoped and hoped would always be happy and that nothing bad would ever happen to her.

The delight drained suddenly from Fee's lovely face. 'Oh Ruthie, you'll forget me! You'll have other friends, Sydney friends, and you'll change, you'll be all different, you won't want me! You'll think, How could I ever have been best friends with that dumb little crybaby Fee?'

'Fiona Lachlan!' said Ruth sternly.

'Oh!' Fee jumped back, startled at the sound of her full name, and the fierce expression on Ruth's face. 'What? What?'

Ruth rushed forward and held her close. 'I'll always be your friend, Fee! Always and always and forever!'

Fee gave a great happy sigh. 'Promise?'

'Promise.'

A whistle blew. 'Time's up!' Fred Wheeler yelled from down the platform.

Ruth flung her arms round Margaret May. 'I want to stay with you!' she whispered.

'Of course you don't,' said Margaret May. And she released Ruth's arms and gently turned her round again towards the train. 'There!' she said, and Ruth felt a firm little push, just beneath her shoulderblades. 'In you go,' said Margaret May.

FOR a long while she sat beside the window, watching the familiar landmarks go by: the silos and the water tower, Anderson's dairy, the showground where the carnival came every New Year. She sat with her face pressed close against the glass that was still warm from a day's travel across the plains, looking and looking and looking – because it was just possible that she might catch a last glimpse of him, of Tam Finn, roaming across the paddocks or wandering the narrow roads that skirted them. The train circled round Barinjii, past the highway and the crossroads where Ruth's mother had died. 'Bye Mum,' she whispered. 'I'm going but I'll come back again.' The wheels rumbled over the bridge, and there was the end of Starlight Lane and Skelly's dam gleaming sullenly in the last of the light, and the Hogans' old house on top of the hill. And there was Helen Hogan in her red dress standing in the backyard, doing nothing, staring out over Barinjiii, as if she was looking for someone, looking and looking and looking . . .

They came to the crossing gates on the Bulga Road where a slight figure in a blue shirt was standing holding a bicycle, waiting for the train to pass. He waved, and for a second, because of the blue shirt and because she'd been looking, hoping to see him, Ruth thought that it was Tam Finn. But as the train sped over the crossing she saw it was a man waiting there; that his hair was grey, and the blue shirt was more faded than Tam Finn's had been.

It was her father. He'd ridden all the way out from town just to wave her goodbye. 'Dad!' she cried, and she waved and waved and her father saw her and a smile broke over his face so that Ruth could see how it was true what Nan said: how he might once have been a laughing, singing kind of boy. Then he was gone. The sun began to sink but she stayed by the window for a long time, watching the light fade away and the country outside grow unfamiliar, so that if she'd got off into the dark she wouldn't have known the way home.

She pulled down the blind and ate the sandwiches Nan had made for her, ham and lettuce, tomatoes and bright yellow cheese, and at nine o'clock the guard came with a cup of tea. He pulled down the bed for her, said, 'Breakfast at five tomorrow morning, sleep well,' and then went out again. Ruth took off her skirt and blouse and hung them on the hanger in the tiny wardrobe, she put on her new dressing gown and slipped into the bathroom across the corridor. She washed her hands in her own small sink with the tiny cake of soap that Fee had admired, and crawled between the stiff cold sheets with NSW Railways printed in blue along the hem. She closed her eyes and at once fell into a strange half-sleep, full of images and dreams and the screech and rattle of the train's speeding wheels: 'Let me, oh, let me, help me, let me, help me,' they sang. Skelly's dam loomed up like a great blank gleaming eye, and she felt Nan's firm hand against the centre of her back and heard her voice saying, 'In you go.'

'She pushed him in,' the train wheels chanted down beneath her, 'pushed him in, him in, him in—'

'No she didn't,' Ruth said sleepily, and the train wheels sang, 'Didn't, didn't, didn't,' and then, going faster, 'Did, did, did.'

'That's just an old story,' Ruth mumbled in her sleep, 'Even Tam Finn said it was.' And the train gave a sudden jerk, and rattled over a long bridge into the dark country on the other side where the wheels began a new song. 'Tam Finn!' they sang, 'Tam Finn, Oh! Tam Finn, Tam Finn, Tam Finn!'

WHEN the old Holden reached the edge of the town, Margaret May leaned forward and said to Mattie, 'Could you let me out here, dear? It's a beautiful evening and I'd like to walk a little, it isn't far to home.'

'She's all by herself now,' said Fee, gazing back through the window as they drove on towards the town.

Margaret May walked on slowly. She took her time – there

was no hurry, she'd prepared cold meat and salad for tea and left it in the fridge for Ray. 'Well, she's gone,' she murmured to herself, and then a little further on, 'Well, she got away.' As she walked the sun sank down below the horizon and stars began to wink and twinkle in the pale greenish sky. A crow called mournfully across the paddocks, and by the time she reached the first streetlamp a cold wind had sprung up, and she shivered and thought, Not much left of summer now. Past the garage she turned left and, out of habit, began to walk up the long slope towards Saint Columba's. The door was open, a soft warm light shone from inside, and Margaret May thought longingly of the little brown Virgin in her corner beneath the window, her calm, impassive face – but she had made a promise to herself in the church that morning, and it was a promise she would keep; she would not go in there again. She would never speak to *him*. She squared her shoulders and walked on.

From the window of the sacristy Father Joseph watched her pass and remembered again that long-ago night when he'd carried her from the hospital, and he thought that the feel of those frail baby bones in his hands had passed into his soul forever. He opened the window and called, 'Maidie! Maidie!' but outside in the twilight the small determined figure kept walking on. She passed beneath the streetlamp and its light shone down on her and he saw for the first time that her hair was white. He hadn't noticed this before; he hadn't even noticed when it had first begun to turn from brown to grey. Five minutes back, if anyone had asked him the colour of Margaret May Gower's hair, he'd have answered unhesitatingly, 'Brown.' As he watched her cross the road away from him he thought, not of their long friendship or how he had betrayed her in the church this morning, or even of the possibility that she might never speak to him again, but of how unutterably strange it was that they should both have become old.

PART TWO

Happiness

one

When she graduated from the university, Ruth left Sydney to study in London. 'London, eh?' her dad marvelled when she'd received the grant that would take her there. 'All that way!'

Ruth hesitated, taking in his skinny figure, the shoulders stooped a little now beneath the old grey pullover, his mild and blameless face. 'I could always stay and teach in Sydney,' she began. 'It'd be closer to you.'

Ray Gower wouldn't have a bar of that. 'You go,' he'd said. 'You go to London, Ruthie. Your nan would have wanted it.' He rubbed his hands together and wagged his head at the wonder of it all. 'By golly she'd have wanted it, eh?'

He was right. Ruth thought of her nan in the garden on that bright morning the Leaving Certificate results had arrived: the almost reverent way she'd held the letter, as if it was some precious object; the fierce, triumphant light in her eyes. 'A girl like you should see the world,' she'd declared.

Nan had died in Ruth's first year at university. Ruth had come back home for the funeral, and all the way up in the train she'd been unable to believe that Nan had really, truly gone. It had to be a mistake, she'd decided; poor Dad had got it all wrong somehow. By the time the train was halfway to Barinjii she'd convinced herself that Nan would be there at the station to meet her, that at this very moment, as the train rolled through the flat country past Orange, Nan would be out in her garden cutting flowers for the little green vase in Ruth's old room. But when she'd stepped out onto the platform her grandmother hadn't been there, only her friend Fee with her new husband Mattie, and one look at their faces had been enough to tell her that her dad's message hadn't been any kind of mistake. It was true: Nan was gone.

Father Joseph had performed the funeral mass. He'd known Nan since she was a baby, and in the graveyard the old man had broken down, collapsing on the dusty grass, his robes spread out round him like a big child's party dress, bawling out that special name he'd had for her, 'Maidie! Maidie!' He'd sounded like a child left all alone. Six months later he'd gone, too.

SO Ruth went to London, studied for her doctorate and became a teacher at the university. When she was thirty-three she'd married Joe, a teacher in the music department. They didn't last long together; two years and she and Joe went their separate ways, amicably, even happily. When she looked back on her brief marriage, Ruth thought that neither she nor Joe had been the marrying kind. Being single suited them best; they were naturally solitary.

But there were other times, especially those nights when she woke from a dream of Barinjii so vivid that the scents of heat and dust and baking grasses seemed to fill her cold little room, when Ruth would think there might be another reason. An imprint of love had been stamped on her heart when she was a girl, an image to which no one else could ever correspond. Tam Finn, she would think, Tan Finn, Tam Finn, Tam Finn, Oh! And she would see his pale narrow face beneath the glossy black curls, the rainy grey eyes gazing into hers, and hear his voice pleading, 'Let me, oh, help me, let me!' She would hear the tune of the old hymn he used to sing, roaming the paddocks of Barinjii, the notes so pure they seemed to promise some perfect loveliness she hadn't been able to grasp and might never ever find: 'the real true thing,' as her nan used to say.

Reading Fee's letters from home, which always ended anxiously, 'And are you happy, Ruthie?' Ruth would answer that yes, she was happy. There were all kinds of happiness: she had her friends and students in London, and Fee and her godchildren back home; she loved her work – and there were so many other small perfect pleasures: a sudden unexpected snowfall in winter, long summer evenings in the garden of her small house, walks beside the river before the sun was up, mist rising from the water, a sky the colour of pearls, an old hymn floating through the doors of the Cathedral: *Come down, O love divine, Seek now this heart of mine—*

There were mornings when Ruth looked out from her bedroom window and felt in love with the whole world. That was happiness, surely; that was the real true thing.

Though she had had no children.

Her friend Sally Fitzgerald had no children either. 'Do you ever wonder what a child of your own would have looked like?' Sally asked her, one cold grey winter's day when they were sitting in Ruth's pretty living room drinking wine and listening to the London rain dripping down onto the sodden bushes and cold fallen leaves.

'No,' Ruth had answered.

'You're lucky then,' said Sally. 'I do, all the time. It's like finding an old book with a page missing, the page that turns out to be the one you most wanted to read.'

Ruth didn't wonder what a child of her own would have looked like because she knew. It would have been a pale-skinned child with glossy black curls and eyes that were the colour of rain. It would have been Tam Finn's child, if he hadn't said to her, that long-ago night in Starlight Lane, 'Well, little schoolteacher, off you go then . . .'

'WHAT happened to Tam Finn?' she asked Fee on her first visit home from London. There they were again, sitting on the edge of the front verandah, swinging their bare feet in the ferns below. The house in Hopeton Street belonged to Fee and Mattie now; Fee's parents had moved to the coast when Mr Lachlan had retired.

'Tam Finn? No one knows really,' said Fee. 'He went off to Sydney ages back, just after that business with Helen Hogan's dad.'

'What business with Helen Hogan's dad?'

'Didn't I write to you about it?'

'No.'

'I thought I had. That's what kids do to you; they take away your brain cells.' Fee settled her spine more comfortably against the verandah post. 'Well, it wasn't all that long after you left for Sydney the first time. The Hogans found out Helen was pregnant and Mr Hogan drove out to *Fortuna* and beat up Tam Finn. Harry Finn wasn't at home but old Mrs Finn was there and they say she just stood watching, and when Mr Hogan was finished with Tam all she said was, "Now get off my property."'

Ruth kicked angrily at the ferns.

Fee looked sideways at her friend. 'So you never saw him down there in Sydney? Tam Finn?'

'Of course I didn't!'

But the thing was, for a long time down in the city, whenever she turned a corner into a new strange street, Ruth had half expected that Tam Finn might suddenly be there. He would be there, and he would walk towards her, smiling, and say, 'Here's Ruthie.' Even in London, walking by the river before the sun was up, she wouldn't have been surprised to see him come walking over the bridge, a solitary figure in the misty morning light. 'Why should I see him down in Sydney?' she asked Fee. 'We hardly knew each other.'

Fee shrugged. 'Oh, stranger things happen.'

'So he didn't come back here? Not once?'

'No,' answered Fee. 'I don't suppose there was any point, really. His dad died, and old Mrs Finn hated Tam. There was nothing for him here – remember how his dad left *Fortuna* to his cousin?'

'You mean that time when he got chucked out of Ag School? When we were kids? You mean his dad never forgave him? Just for that?'

'They're hard people, the Finns. Remember old Mrs Finn? She's still going strong, would you believe? Still living out at *Fortuna*, with the cousin's family.'

There was a silence, then Fee said, 'They shot the peacock, you know.'

'What?'

'The peacock, the one they used to have in the garden at *Fortuna*. They shot it.'

'Tam Finn's peacock? Why? Why did they do that?'

'The cousin said it made too much noise.'

'Dancer,' whispered Ruth.

'Was that its name?'

'Yes.' Ruth brushed a straggling lock of hair behind her ear. Her hand was trembling. 'Someone told me, I don't remember who.'

'Ah,' said Fee. 'Poor old Tam Finn, eh? He lost everything.'

'You didn't like him back when we were kids.'

'Well, that's just it, we were *kids*; we didn't know anything much.'

'No,' said Ruth, and looked down sadly into the ferns.

'You had a bit of a crush on him, didn't you?'

'Me?'

'Yes, *you*. I could tell. That last summer, before you went away.'

'You never said anything.'

'I never said anything because you'd never have admitted

it. And you'd have been mad with me; no one likes having their crushes pointed out to them.'

It hadn't been a crush, thought Ruth. It had been a mixture of curiosity, and fascination, and lust, all of which she'd been too young to understand – just as she'd been too young to understand that look of desolation in his eyes; it had simply frightened her, like Helen Hogan had frightened her, down by the creek in her red dress that was the colour of blood.

The funny thing was how the fascination was still there. 'I didn't have a crush on him,' she said, and knew that she would never admit to that fascination, which might even be a strange kind of love, not even to her best friend, not even when they were old. She would never admit it to anyone if it couldn't be to him.

'What happened to Helen Hogan?' she asked.

'I don't know. She went off to Sydney – to have the baby, I suppose.'

'And she never came back?'

'Never. And neither did Kathy Ryan, remember her? She was one of Tam Finn's girls. And Ellie Lester?'

Ruth saw them, a trio of girls: one fair, one dark, one auburn haired, like a procession of princesses in a fairy story. They'd all be middle aged now; they'd most likely be married, with other children.

'You're the only one of Tam Finn's girls who came back again,' said Fee.

'I *wasn't* one of Tam Finn's girls!'

Almost though, thought Ruth. She'd almost been one of them.

'Lucky you weren't,' said Fee, 'seeing as the three of them disappeared. You know what I reckon?'

'What?'

'I reckon that if they ever drain Skelly's dam they're going to find bones down there. And they won't be sheep and cattle.'

Two

By the time she was thirty, Fee had five children, all boys, all Ruth's godchildren: Matthew and David, Mark and Louis, and, last of all, Josh.

'*Five* boys!' Ruth marvelled, back home for Josh's christening, holding her new godchild in her arms. 'So many!'

Fee laughed and Mattie said, 'Well, see, it's this way: we kept on trying for a girl because we wanted to call her Ruth . . .'

Five boys. For Fee it was a life. There was hardly time to think: it was all rush and clamour, the days filled up, they brimmed and rolled away, flowed into weeks and months and years. There were first steps and first words and first days at school, paintings on the fridge door, home-made cards with *Happy Mother's Day* spelled out in glitter, wobbly clay cats and dogs along the windowsills. Before they knew it, high school had arrived: sports days and swimming carnivals, dances and girlfriends, old cars, exams, and leaving home.

Fee was happy. You could see it in the brightness of her face and hear it in her laughing voice. Children called out to her in the street, 'Hello, Mrs Howe!', adults smiled; everyone loved Fee. 'It does me good just to see you, Fee,' Ruth's dad would say whenever she came into the shop. And sometimes in the evenings when the boys were all in bed, she'd look up from her book or her mending or the letter she was writing to Ruth and catch Mattie gazing at her at her from across the room – 'Little one,' he'd whisper, and then Fee would jump up from her chair and run to him so quickly, so lightly, you'd think she was a girl.

Walking the familiar streets of Barinjii, where nothing much had changed, crossing the playground on her way to collect the smallest child, Fee would often think of Ruth: Ruth far away in London, studying, teaching, Ruth married and then not married, single again, Ruth at forty, without a child. 'Do you think you'll get married again?' Fee wrote anxiously, because sometimes she felt she couldn't bear that Ruth should be alone. 'Probably not,' Ruth replied cheerfully. 'But look, I'm happy, Fee. Honestly. There are all kinds of happiness, you know – different kinds for different people, mine is just different from yours.'

All kinds of happiness. But Fee wanted Ruth to have really loved someone and been loved back in return, perfectly – and this someone didn't seem to have been her husband, Joe, about whom Ruth spoke so casually you'd think he'd been only a friend. There'd been no one she'd cared about at Barinjii – but whenever Fee thought this, she'd pause, and frown – because had there been someone she didn't know about? Had there been something going on between Ruth and Tam Finn in that last summer before Ruth went down to Sydney University? It seemed impossible: Ruth and *Tam Finn*! And that was the time he'd been getting around with Helen Hogan, anyway –

not that two girls at once would have been a problem for *him*! But Ruth always looked so *conscious* when his name came up, even now – and she'd known the peacock's name, which no one else had, ever. Fee remembered that day they'd got their exam results; how she'd come back from Dubbo and found Ruth on the verandah, and you could tell she'd been crying. Had *that* been about Tam Finn? No, thought Fee, no it couldn't have been – because if Ruth had been seeing Tam Finn, even for a single day, surely everyone in Barinjii would have known!

RUTH'S letters came in long blue airmail envelopes. Wavy lines, like a child's drawing of the sea, flowed over the stamps in the right-hand corner, and a postmark which said, London, SW1.

London. When Ruth had first told her she was going there, Fee had found it difficult to take in. London was a place you read about in books and newspapers, a place you saw in films and on the television, a place that well-off people visited when they retired. But to live there! For years and years! So that it was like your home!

'Oh, I'd never think of London as home,' Ruth said once on a visit. 'Not proper home. Even if I stayed there forever.'

'Oh don't!' Fee had whispered. 'Don't stay there forever!'

'Of course I won't! But wherever I live, I'll always think of Barinjii as home.'

London. The word itself had a kind of magic. Fee spoke it aloud in the quiet house when Mattie was at work and the kids at school. 'London', she would say softly, standing at the kitchen window, staring out over the backyard, at the old shed and the peppercorn trees and the paddocks beyond the sagging fence. She remembered the day of the exam results again, how she'd begged Ruth to open the envelope because she'd been too scared, she remembered how bright the sun had been that afternoon, glaring in through this very window, and how, when she'd snatched the blind down, Ruth had given a little jump and said, 'Oh!'

And then a few weeks after, Ruth had gone to Sydney and then off to London while Fee stayed at home. 'I love it here where I've always been,' she'd said to Ruth that afternoon in the kitchen. If you could go back in time, Fee wondered, if it could be that very day again, would she feel the same?

She did love it here, of course she did.

Only —

Only what?

She didn't know.

Ruth's house was in a place called Pimlico. Pimlico, SW1. 'It's shabby,' she wrote, 'little narrow streets and council flats and little narrow houses. But I love it – it's near the river and I can walk there in the mornings. And it's close to most places: I could walk to Westminster Abbey if I wanted to marry Prince Charles, or to Buckingham Palace if I wanted to have tea with the Queen! But I guess I'll stay single, in which case, it's so easy to get to work from here —'

On a rare trip to Sydney, Fee went into a big bookstore and bought a London street directory. In quiet moments back home, she'd sit out on the verandah and turn the pages to

Pimlico, SW1; she'd run her finger along Lilac Street, which was Ruth's street; then trace her route down to the river, to Westminster Abbey and the Palace; then over the pages to Bloomsbury and the university.

'We can go there one day, you know,' said Mattie, discovering her out on the verandah one summer evening, dreaming, the directory open on her lap.

'Go where?'

'London. When the kids are all grown up.' He grinned at her. 'Grown up and off our hands.'

'They'll never be.'

'Sooner than you think!' He waved towards the front gate where the youngest was swinging, singing a small wordless song. 'He'll be off to school next year, be at university before you know it.'

'Josh?' Fee shook her head at him. 'He's only five.'

'Before you know it,' Mattie had repeated, hunkering down beside her, his big warm arm sliding round her shoulders, his kiss like a solid promise on her cheek.

TIME flowed on. Ruth's dad sold his store and settled in at the new retirement village in Dubbo; the Hogans moved further west and their old house on the hill above Skelly's dam remained empty, the doors and windows boarded, a loose sheet of iron clattering in the wind. Fee walked down Starlight Lane one windy afternoon and remembered Helen Hogan in the playground way back in primary school telling them scary stories beneath the peppercorn trees. '*But what if you don't know who you really are?'* she'd chanted eerily. The words sounded so clearly in Fee's mind that for a moment she thought Helen was behind her, right there in the lane. She swung round, but of course there was no one. How could there be? Helen had grown up and gone to Sydney long ago. Out in the paddock the wind rippled the dark water of the dam, and she remembered how Ruth had been scared to walk past that place because it was where her granddad had drowned. People still said Don Gower's ghost walked in the paddock, the dead calf tucked beneath his arm.

Fee's children were all grown now. Matthew and David were married, Mark had a job in Melbourne, Louis was teaching out at Broken Hill. Josh was still at home, but that was only for a little while; at the end of summer he'd be heading off to Sydney University.

Josh was her favourite. People said parents shouldn't have favourites, but how could you help it, children were people, weren't they?

'Who do you love best?' the boys would clamour when they were little, clustering round her, pulling at her skirt and hands. 'Who?'

'I love you all the same,' she'd tell them.

Josh was the only one who'd never asked. He'd come to their bedroom early, before his older brothers were awake, and stand silently next to Fee's side of the bed. Sensing his steady gaze even through her sleep, she'd wake and see his small face, a pale glimmer in the dusky room, his big eyes fixed on hers. 'Here I am,' he'd say.

He was the odd one out amongst the boys: Matthew and

David were mates; the middle ones, Mark and Louis, were inseparable as twins; Josh, three years younger, was on his own. He even looked different, small and slender and dark-haired, while the others were big-boned and sturdy, ruddy-cheeked and fair. They were noisy, he was quiet, a little air of loneliness clinging round him.

She worried about him as she'd never worried about the older boys. She slept uneasily when he went away on camps and school trips, dreaming of accidents; of drowning and snakebite and a child lost out in the bush. She'd be washing the tea things and see the bus smashed in the middle of the road. She trembled when the note arrived for camp, though she signed it anyway; you had to, you had to learn to let them go. And when the homecoming bus pulled in at the school gates and the little crowd of waiting mothers surged forward, Fee would stand at the back of them, unsmiling, her heart already cold with dread, she was so certain he wouldn't be there. In her dreams this had happened many times: the dream bus would spill out its children and sit empty by the gates, its seats and aisles laid bare. 'Where's Josh?' Fee would cry, circling round and round it, running up and down the verge, but it was obvious from the blank faces of the parents and teachers that no one had ever heard of her child.

In the real world Josh always came safely home. Straggling down the steps behind the others, foraging in the boot for his belongings, he'd avert his eyes from his mother until that last moment when he'd turn slowly, backpack in one hand, sleeping-bag in the other, and say, 'Well, here I am.' These days there was a note of accusation in the words, as if he knew all about Fee's anxious dreams and despised her for them.

Boys were like that, of course; the older boys had been the same. As they grew bigger they were fierce for independence, mothers were an embarrassment. It had seemed funny with the others, endearing, she and Mattie had laughed about it in the privacy of their room. With Josh it was in deadly earnest, like a knife stuck into her heart. Sometimes she thought he hated her.

Even with favourites you had to let them go. You had to let them go so they could be happy; it didn't matter about you. Fee thought of Ruth's nan standing on the platform of Barinjii station, watching Ruth's train disappear down the line. She remembered how the old lady had asked to get out of the car as they reached the first streets of the town, how Fee had looked back and seen the small figure walking slowly, all by herself, forever lonely, up the same old hill.

At seventeen, Josh was a thin gangly boy with a distant manner, who seemed older than his age. He was clever at school, wrapped up in maths and physics, chemistry. 'Not just clever, exceptional,' his teachers said. He was sitting for the Higher School Certificate, he'd win a scholarship to Sydney, the teachers told them, and after that he might go anywhere.

'You work too hard,' Fee said, noticing the pale mauve shadows underneath his eyes.

'It's not work, Mum,' he answered.

'What is it, then?' she asked him, and Josh went quiet for a moment before he replied, with a deep seriousness that made his voice tremble, 'It's *seeing*, Mum, it's learning how to see.' His eyes shone with the discovery. And Fee remembered the way Ruth's pen had flown over the page in the examinations; her face alight with exactly this kind of joy. 'There are all kinds of happiness,' her best friend had written, and this was obviously Josh's kind. He would win his scholarship, he would go away. Perhaps one day he would be famous; he would see all the places Fee had never seen. And she would stay at home again.

BY the middle of that summer Fee was glad he was going away. Josh, who'd never got round to having a girlfriend, had suddenly taken up with Lou Harker, a skimpy little thing, one of a large family who lived in an old weatherboard far out along the Toongi Road. People said her grandmother had been a beauty, that Harry Finn, Tam's father, had been wild about her for a little while, and that she was the reason Tam's mother had run away from *Fortuna*. People in Barinjii would say anything, Fee knew, but Lou Harker definitely had a look of the Finns about her: that blue-black crow's wing hair, those wide-set, slatey grey eyes. She was nineteen, two years older than Josh, and he'd met her in the big newsagent's in Dubbo, where she'd worked since she'd left school. Now he was on the bus to Dubbo every afternoon, just so he could ride back with her after work. At the weekends he simply disappeared.

They hardly saw him. He'd won his scholarship, he was due to leave for Sydney at the end of February, but the reading lists sent on by the university lay untouched and gathering dust on the desk in his room. It seemed he'd forgotten all about *seeing*, Fee thought bitterly – his eyes were fixed blindly on Lou.

'He's going to throw it all away!' she wailed to Mattie.

Mattie was imperturbable as ever. 'He'll be okay.'

'No, he won't; she's out to catch him.'

'Things'll cool off when he goes down to Sydney, you'll see.'

'They won't, I bet,' said Fee. She'd seen the determination in the girl's eyes. 'She'll find some way to stop him.'

'Josh's got more sense than that.'

'Sense! She's got him wrapped round her little finger!'

A week before Josh was due to leave, Mattie and Fee were sitting in the kitchen drinking tea. Apart from the teapot and their cups and saucers, the table was cleared; the dishes had been washed and put away. Josh hadn't come home for tea. 'He said he'd be back,' mourned Fee, 'he *promised* me.' An image of Lou Harker's narrow face rose up before her. 'Don't go,' the girl would have whispered. 'Stay here with me.' Fee's full lips compressed themselves into a thin hard line and Mattie, who was watching her, thought how in all the years they'd been married he'd never seen such a mean expression on her sweet face.

'Ah, he's young, Fee,' he said softly.

'Well, that's just it, he's *too* young, he'll—' she broke off, and they both looked up, because outside in the quiet summer night the front gate had squealed open and then clanged shut and footsteps were coming along the front path and up the steps onto the verandah. *Two* sets of footsteps! And through the open front door a girl's voice sounded gently but very firmly, 'It's going to all right, Josh. Everything. I promise.'

Who was *she* to promise? Fee began to get up from her chair but Mattie put a hand on her arm and she sat down again.

The screen door rattled. The footsteps sounded louder on the polished wooden floors. Halfway across the living room they stopped. 'Everything,' the girl's voice said again, and then there was a small perfect silence in which Fee and Mattie heard the unmistakable sound of a kiss. A moment later, Josh appeared in the kitchen doorway, holding tight to Lou Harker's hand.

Those slatey eyes took in Fee and Mattie at a glance, a glance which said, quite clearly, 'I'm not scared of *you*.' As for Josh, his face was flushed and his hair was mussed about. He didn't beat about the bush. 'Mum, Dad,' he said, 'Lou and I are getting married.'

The silence that followed could have been one of shock, except that Fee, at least, had been expecting something like this. Marriage would be the skimpy girl's intention, her brilliant, shining goal. It was Mattie who seemed stunned by the announcement, one big hand coming down on the table: *whump!* Cups rattled in their saucers, the teapot trembled. He looked at Fee, who looked – she couldn't help herself, even though she knew it was way too early for anything to show – straight at the girl's belly. Not that there was one: Lou Harker was thin as a stick. 'Straight up and down as a drink of water,' as Fee's grandma would have said, and Fee was granted a sudden incandescent vision of herself at seventeen, clad in white satin, smoothing a hand over the new soft swell of flesh beneath her waist. And her grandma Milly's kind eyes smiling into hers, and her own young voice whispering, 'Don't tell them, all right?' And Gran's sweet vanished voice replying, 'As if I'd tell.'

Mattie had been following the direction of Fee's gaze, and when he realised its purpose his cheeks flamed with embarrassment.

Josh glowered at the pair of them. 'It isn't *that*,' he snarled. 'That's not the reason.'

'No it isn't,' said the girl, and her lips twitched slightly, as if she found Josh's old parents funny. She caught the boy's eye and very slightly nodded. Go on, she was telling him.

Josh stepped closer to the table. 'Anyway,' he said accusingly, 'what about you two?'

'Eh?'

'Don't come the innocent, Dad! You know what I mean.'

'Know what you mean? I haven't got a bloody clue, mate. Speak plain!'

'Twenty-first of April, 1959,' said Josh. 'That plain enough?'

Mattie blinked. 'Our wedding day,' whispered Fee. Beneath the tablecloth she reached for his hand. She knew what was coming. The skimpy girl had made Josh merciless.

'And December the nineteenth, same year?' he went on. 'That one sound familiar?'

Fee and Mattie looked down at the table. December nineteenth was their first child's birthday.

Josh raised a hand to his forehead and closed his eyes in mock concentration. 'Let's see, now. April twenty-first till December nineteenth: if I'm calculating right, that's eight months, nearly. Stork come early, did he, Dad?'

'You little devil!' Mattie jumped to his feet, one hand balled into a fist. Fee pulled him down again.

Josh moved back a little. 'Sorry,' he said.

'Like hell you are!'

'Look, Dad, how do you think Lou feels with you two staring at her like that? Thinking she's' – a bright flush spread over his thin cheeks – 'thinking she's *expecting*!' he finished in a rush, and then turned to the girl and murmured tenderly, 'Sorry, Lou.'

'S'all right,' said Lou.

Josh kissed Lou Harker. She kissed him back.

Fee and Mattie waited.

'Anyway, like I told you,' Josh continued, turning back to them at last, 'that's not the reason Lou and I are getting married. It's because I'm going down to Sydney and we want to be together.'

'Together!' Mattie muttered hoarsely, and he put his head in his hands as if it had become too heavy for his neck to hold upright.

Fee took over. 'But where will you live?' she asked them. 'You can't live in student accommodation if you're married. It wouldn't be allowed.'

'Allowed!' sneered Josh. 'Think we haven't thought of that, Mum? Think we're babies? Think we can't work things out for ourselves?'

The girl spoke. 'We've got a place,' she told them.

Mattie raised his head. 'You've got a place?'

'My Aunty Brenda down in Sydney. In Five Dock.' She spoke the name of the suburb with a little air of pride. 'She's got this bungalow in her backyard, she says we can have it, free. It just needs doing up a bit, and Uncle Jim, he says he'll give us a hand, you know.'

Fee and Mattie's faces took on identical expressions. They knew all right. Lou Harker's family had stolen a march on them.

'And that'll do us fine,' said Josh, and he kissed the skimpy girl again, on the top of her small dark head. The kiss made a neat little sound. It was like a full stop to something; it was like telling Mattie and Fee they weren't allowed to argue.

Only they couldn't keep it in. 'And just how are you going to support a – a wife' – Mattie stumbled on the word, he couldn't seem to get the sense of it, not with Josh in mind – 'on a scholarship?'

'Nothing's cheap down there, you know,' said Fee.

They sneered at her.

'Free bungalow or not,' growled Mattie.

Josh threw back his head defiantly. 'I'll get a part-time job, work nights.'

'And what about your studies?'

'I'll manage,' said Josh. 'Like I always have.'

As if *they'd* been stopping him, thought Fee furiously. As if they'd made him chop wood and clean the fowl house so he didn't have time to study. As if she and Mattie had been making such a racket that their son couldn't hear his own thoughts.

'You'll be too tired, son,' said Mattie. 'The only kind of job you'd get down there is going to make you dead on your feet. All you'll want to do is sleep.'

The girl stepped forward. She came right up to the table and put her hand on it, as if to hold her steady. '*I'll* work,' she said. '*I'll* support us, there's jobs going for girls like me, Aunty Brenda says. Waitressing, shopwork. I've got experience.'

Fee stared at the hand there on the table. It was a very small hand, but it looked quite strong and fierce right there beside their floral crockery.

Lou saw her looking and snatched her hand away. 'We won't starve, don't *you* worry about *us*. And don't worry about Josh, he won't get *tired*, *I'll* look after him. We'll do fine, just you wait and see!' She put both hands on her hips and glared at them defiantly.

Mattie struggled to hide a sudden grin. Fee scowled at him; he was supposed to be on *her* side. She wanted to slap him, and slap the skimpy girl as well. As for her favourite son, the *genius*, the boy who wanted to *see* – 'We'll see all right,' she told him grimly. 'We'll see you mess up your life, throw away your chances, just for—'

Josh didn't let her finish. 'C'mon Lou!' he said, grabbing at the girl's thin arm. 'I'm not staying here tonight! Or – or ever! I'd rather sleep in Perry's orchard, where the air is *clean*!' He swung away from them and rushed from the room, hurrying Lou beside him. Fee jumped up and ran after them, across the living room, down the hall where the doors of the big blanket cupboard were already wide open, and Josh was grabbing up a sleeping-bag.

Their sleeping-bag, Fee saw, the big double one that she and Mattie used for camping trips.

'Put that back at once!'

'No!'

'Give it to *me*!' They struggled briefly. The girl looked away. A corner of the bag flicked across Fee's cheek.

Josh didn't even stay to see if it had hurt. 'C'mon, Lou!' They rushed right past her.

At the front door she howled after them, 'But where are you *going*?' Night had come. It was dark out there. A cold wind was blowing.

'I *told* you!' bawled Josh from the footpath. 'I'm going to sleep in Perry's orchard.'

'And me!' cried the skimpy girl. 'I'm going to sleep in Perry's orchard too! With him!'

'But – but it's dark,' Fee cried helplessly.

Josh swung back towards her. 'That's all right, Mum,' he yelled. 'I'm a big boy now; I'm not afraid of the dark!'

'HE'LL ruin his chances!' wept Fee to Mattie in the darkness of their bedroom. 'They'll be crammed up together in that tiny shack—'

'We don't know it's tiny, love.'

'Bungalows are always tiny. They'll be crammed up, Mattie, and Josh'll be exhausted, working in some factory, he won't be able to study—'

'It won't come to that, love. We'll help them out.'

Neither of them mentioned the possibility that Lou Harker might fade away from Josh's life; it was so obvious that the skimpy girl wasn't the type to fade. Colourfast, thought Fee bitterly. 'They'll start having children,' she panicked, voice rising, 'he'll give it all up, those things he's good at – the physics, the maths, it'll all go; he'll be just *ordinary*. He'll never go anywhere! He'll be *stuck*!'

The word had weight and resonance. It was like something unholy, a small bomb dropped inside the room. It was Fee home forever with the children and never going anywhere, never finding the person she might have been, if she hadn't got married so young. And through the darkness Fee could sense Mattie thinking all this as well – she sensed the quiver of his hurt and sorrow and shame. 'Oh!' she whispered. 'Oh.'

He turned on his side, away. 'Oh, Mattie!' she said. 'I didn't mean me.' She pressed herself close to him, hiding her face against his broad, warm back. 'I didn't mean *I* felt stuck.' Then she had to be honest. 'Or at least, only a little part of me. A really, really little bit.'

He turned and held her close, wordlessly.

'I've been so happy, Mattie.' And suddenly she knew it. Of course she'd been happy; she'd had the real true thing. She grasped his face in her hands and covered it with kisses. '*You're* the real true thing,' she whispered.

'YOU know, love,' Mattie said a little while later, 'I think—'

'What do you think?' she smiled into his shoulder.

'Well, once Josh and, ah—'

'Lou.'

'Yeah. Lou.' He grinned. Fee stopped smiling.

'Once Josh and Lou are settled, perhaps we could take that trip to London—'

Fee propped herself up on one elbow and looked down at him. 'Settled,' she murmured. 'As if anyone ever was.' She sighed and lay back, watching the leaf shadows from the big gum dancing on the ceiling. Out there in Perry's orchard the wind would be tossing in the trees. Cold.

'I'm not sure I want to go to London anymore,' she said to Mattie.

'But what about visiting Ruth?'

'I had a letter today. Ruth's thinking of coming back here, if she can get a job at Sydney University. She wants to see more of her dad.'

'Ah.'

'It's Josh I want to go places.'

'And he's going to,' promised Mattie. 'You can bet on that.'

'Good.'

They lay there silently for a moment, then Mattie spoke again. 'Fee?'

'Yes?'

'The thing is, Fee, about them, about Josh and, um, Lou—'

'What? What about them?'

'Josh isn't going to ruin his chances; he's not that kind of boy. And that Lou—'

'Yes?' Fee's voice was cool.

'That Lou looks like she wouldn't let him ruin his chances either. Not for anything.'

Fee turned her head a little so he wouldn't see the gleam of jealousy in her eyes.

'You've got to—'

'Got to what?' she snapped. 'What have I got to do?'

He took her hand and kissed it. 'You've got to have some trust.'

LONG after Mattie had fallen asleep Fee lay awake beside him, thinking of Josh and the girl out there in Perry's orchard, the wind roaring in the trees above them, damp rising through the layers of the sleeping-bag. The trees in the orchard were old and dry – a branch could fall. Had they checked for spiders in the leaf litter? Snakes? Had they—

They. She was saying *they*, as if Josh and Lou Harker were a real couple; as if the skimpy girl was part of the family, as if she was a fact. But Lou Harker was a fact, you could *sense* it: she was there for good.

Tears sprang into Fee's eyes. She slipped from the covers, crept into the bathroom and scrambled into her clothes. Then she too rushed out into the windy night.

There was no moon yet, but the stars were huge, flooding the streets of Barinjii with a gentle silvery light. As she rushed down Hopeton Street, across the windswept park and on through the schoolyard towards the old orchard, Fee couldn't help – whatever Mattie said – the sense of loss for Josh's marvellous future creeping over her again, his brilliant chances winking out like streetlights in an ordinary dawn. So that the orchard appeared through a veil of tears, suddenly, before she was quite ready for it, like some surprising image from a dream. The wind was wilder here, the old trees thrashed and struggled; she walked into them with her arms held protectively above her head.

The big moon had risen now and she found the sleeping-bag easily, in the centre of a clearing, well away from the threat of falling branches, spread neatly like a big picnic tablecloth on the grass. There was no sign of Josh and Lou.

She knelt down and pulled the bag sideways; they'd cleared the leaf litter where spiders might hide, and the ground was firm and dry. The wind dropped suddenly, the air went smooth as silk; somewhere further off she heard a whisper, a giggle, a long broken sigh, and she sprang up guiltily, peering into the shadowy trees. She saw them almost at once, in another small clearing, standing close, their arms around each other, oblivious and unaware. She noticed how the top of Lou's head reached Josh's collarbone, how his chin grazed the top of that blue-black crow's wing hair. She saw the girl raise her face to his, and Josh's lips come gently down on hers.

Fee had stood with Mattie like that, beneath these same old trees. She'd been sixteen. The joy of it! The sheer and perfect happiness! 'Happiness!' she whispered, and though it was only one word and her voice was very soft, Josh and Lou heard her and sprang apart.

'Mum?'

'Oh! I'm sorry,' said Fee. 'Sorry, I – you must think I'm spying, but it isn't that, honestly.'

They gazed at her silently.

'I came because, um – because I wanted to say sorry for what happened back home.'

Still they said nothing, and Fee crept towards them over the uneven ground, stumbling slightly, so that Lou unexpectedly leaped forwards and took her arm. Fee straightened, startled, and their eyes were on a level. 'We,' Fee began, 'I mean, Mattie and I – your dad,' she said, nodding across at Josh, 'we used to come here too. When we first met, when—' She turned back to Lou. 'I was only sixteen,' she gasped. 'And I was so happy, just like you two, and – look, I'm sorry for all that stuff I said back there in the house, I didn't have the right. There are all kinds of happiness, there's all different kinds—' She heard her voice ringing out into the night and thought it sounded like a toddler's voice, a tiny little kid pointing to a window full of Easter eggs, chocolate ones and sugar ones, huge eggs and tiny ones, eggs wrapped in shining foil or nestled in a china cart pulled by a china bunny and crying out, 'There's all different kinds!'

She swallowed. 'All different kinds,' she repeated in a firmer, adult voice, 'and – and no one has the right to tell anyone else which is theirs. And yours is precious, and I'm sorry if I sounded like I didn't think it was.'

'No, it's all right,' said Josh quickly. 'It's okay, Mum.' His eyes sought the girl's. 'It is, isn't it, Lou?'

Lou looked at him and didn't speak. She looked at Fee. They waited for her. They waited humbly.

The girl frowned. Her eyes left their faces and travelled upwards, considering the stars.

Still they waited. Her eyes swept down from the heavens and considered them. Finally she nodded. 'Course it's all right,' she said. 'Anyone can lose their rag.'

Fee's fists clenched by her sides and then opened slowly again.

'And you're right, Mrs Howe,' Lou went on. 'There *are*

all different kinds of happiness. But just because you have one kind, it doesn't mean you can't have others. We can get married and Josh can still do his work—'

'Oh, you're right!' said Fee eagerly.

The wind was very gentle now, no more than a breeze. She noticed how the moonlight threw leaf shadows over their faces and how their bodies inclined towards each other, over the small space between. 'You've got,' Fee began, and then swallowed, and swallowed again, 'the real true thing,' she finished, and looked Lou Harker straight in the eye.

Lou looked back. She smiled at Fee. It was a nice smile.

Then Fee took Josh's hand gently and placed it round Lou's thin back, in which you could feel every knob in the spine. Didn't her mother ever feed her? She took Lou's hands and placed them round Josh's strong neck, where they were obviously meant to be. Then she touched each child lightly on the top of their head, urging their faces together.

'Mum—' protested Josh, but Lou's glance slid sideways and she winked at Fee.

Fee hurried home through the Barinjii summer night. She skipped lightly down the hill and skimmed across the school-yard where she and Ruth had played beneath the peppercorn trees. 'But what if you don't know who you really are?' Helen Hogan's ghostly voice was taunting.

'But I do,' retorted Fee. 'I do know who I am. I'm a happy person, that's me.' She felt light as a feather, light as thistle-down, light as a summer breeze. She felt all of sixteen.

PART THREE

The Real True Thing

one

Ruth woke and the girl was standing over her, motionless beside the bed. She was a skinny girl with thin limbs and big hands and feet at the end of them, like an awkward puppy that would one day grow into a big, big dog. Her pale face was heart-shaped and her eyes were like sad grey stars beneath the glossy blue-black fringe. She didn't say anything when she saw that Ruth had woken, she simply kept on standing there, and her grey eyes, so deeply familiar that they brought a sad little ache to Ruth's heart, were quite expressionless. She could have been looking at any old thing: a jug on a table, a caterpillar crawling along a leaf, a piece of meat on the butcher's slab, waiting for the knife.

Despite her skinnyness and the almost translucent pallor of her skin, the girl was young and strong.

Ruth was getting on. Last birthday she'd turned sixty. '*Sixty!*' her best friend Fee had exclaimed. 'I wouldn't have believed it possible, would you? That *we* could ever be sixty!'

'Unnatural, that's what it is,' Ruth had replied.

A SILENCE filled the big bedroom of the house at the end of Hayfield Lane, which was all by itself and a long way from anywhere.

Ruth lay perfectly still, but you could see she was breathing. Sometimes you could be afraid to breathe, the girl thought; it had happened to her many times. Dancey, her name was. Dancey Trelawny. Helen was her birth name, the one on the forms Ruth had signed, but the girl had said she didn't like it. 'Dancey's my *real* name,' she'd told Ruth.

Since her early retirement Ruth had cared for several children; she was what they called an 'emergency placement', until a more permanent arrangement could be found for children who had no one. 'Though in this case,' the social worker had said with a long thin sigh, 'a permanent arrangement might be a long time coming.'

'You mean?'

'Oh, she's not violent, nothing like that,' Sandy Jimpson had said quickly, 'just a little – strange. Quiet. She's very quiet. And she never smiles. Some people find that disconcerting.'

There was very little in Dancey Trelawny's history to make her smile, Ruth had thought. She was the child of a woman called Tammy Trelawny, a single mother with addiction problems who'd followed an American boyfriend to the States when Dancey was eleven. After a few months the boyfriend had abandoned them, a new one had come along and Dancey had run off, hitched northwards, and joined a street family in Portland. She'd stayed with them almost six months before making her way back to her mother's squat in San Francisco. They'd returned to Sydney and two weeks later Tammy

Trelawny had died of an overdose. Since then Dancey had been moving between temporary placements and residential homes; twice she'd run away.

'That's her,' Sandy Jimpson had said suddenly, pointing through the window of her office, and Ruth had looked out and seen a thin, dark-haired girl sitting by herself on a bench in the garden, so near to them that if the window had been open the girl would have heard every word. And perhaps she had, because she'd looked up at them, and that was when, across that small distance, Ruth had seen that Dancey Trelawny's eyes were that same rainy grey as Tam Finn's.

Ruth had signed the papers and taken Dancey home.

'YOU were sound asleep,' Dancey said now, and her voice held a trace of incredulity, as if it was a wonder to her how anyone in the world could sleep sound.

'That walk home last night must have tired me out,' yawned Ruth, and was puzzled to see a sudden tide of colour spread across the girl's pale cheeks.

Dancey turned sideways and then put up a hand to hide the blush. Almost immediately she took the hand away, because what did she care if Ruth saw and wondered? Let her! What did she care about anyone? She stared sullenly at the two framed photographs which stood side by side on the chest of drawers beside the bed.

There were photographs of Ruth's grandmother and her mother. Margaret May and Polly.

There was no picture of Ruth's dad. The photograph of

Margaret May as a young woman had probably been taken by her friend Father Joseph; Ruth had found it in her nan's special box after her grandmother had died.

Dancey picked it up. 'Who's this?'

'That's my nan. Her name was Margaret May.'

'Margaret Ma-ay,' repeated Dancey in a singsong voice. She studied the face behind the glass, and she thought it was a face that looked out at you, straight.

'She looks a bit like you,' she said to Ruth, though grudgingly, as if, even in saying something as ordinary as this, she might be giving a little of herself away.

'You think so?' Ruth smiled. She sat up and threw her hair back over her shoulders, as if Dancey's remark had made her eager to start the day. It was young hair, the girl noticed. Heavy. Hardly any grey.

'Nan was my favourite person,' said Ruth.

Dancey said nothing, and Ruth considered her stern profile, the straight forehead and elegant nose, the determined tilt of the chin. She thought how there was nothing childish in it.

Dancey put the photograph back down on the chest of drawers and said, 'She looks brave, your nan.'

'She was brave,' agreed Ruth, remembering Margaret May's childhood in the orphanage, the years skivvying out at *Fortuna*, the marriage of which she had never spoken. She reached for the photograph and looked into it: Nan was in her garden, sitting on the wooden bench; behind her heavy roses bloomed along the wall. 'She had the most beautiful garden,' Ruth said softly, remembering the feel of warm sandy paths beneath her bare feet, the scents of thyme and basil, the humming of bees and the squabble of magpies, a lone cicada singing from high up in the gumtree.

'I know a garden,' the girl whispered.

'You do?' It was difficult to imagine where in Dancey's blighted history this garden might have been. 'Was it in America?' Ruth asked gently.

'America?' For a moment the girl looked bewildered, then she said, 'Oh no, it wasn't *there*.' She touched the smooth skin of one temple, and added in a sudden rush, 'It's got a lake with pink waterlilies, and big old trees, and—' Her voice trembled, her hand rushed to her mouth as if she'd said too much.

'A dream garden,' said Ruth, smiling, thinking how Dancey's dream garden sounded like the image she'd had of Tam Finn's garden at *Fortuna*, and how, in those first lonely weeks after she'd left Barinjii, she'd dream of walking there with him.

'It's not a dream garden,' said Dancey, as if she had to make this very clear. 'It's real. It's *somewhere*, in a real place, only I don't know where.'

'Perhaps you'll find it some day,' said Ruth, and then they both fell silent, as if there was some mutual agreement to leave the subject of gardens alone.

Ruth put the photograph of Margaret May back on the bedside table. 'She'd have liked you,' she said to Dancey.

The girl's head jerked round. 'No, she wouldn't!' For a second the grey eyes blazed at Ruth, then they swerved away. 'And anyway, I wouldn't have wanted her to! I don't need people to like me!'

Ruth made no response. She was treading her way cautiously through the wilderness that was Dancey, seeking steady ground. The girl had only been with her for two months.

Though that was longer than she'd been anywhere. 'And she hasn't run away!' Sandy Jimpson had exclaimed delightedly.

'I didn't lock her up,' Ruth had replied.

A sudden breeze rattled the blind, sending a swirl of warm air into the room. A blue shirt thrown carelessly across the back of a chair fluttered for a moment and then went still. Ruth glanced at the clock and saw that it was only ten to seven.

'Hot again,' observed Dancey, her face once more expressionless. She reached for the second photograph. It was the one of Polly which had sat on the mantelpiece in the house at Barinjii. The girl stared down at the beautiful face. 'Who's *this*?' she whispered.

'My mother.'

'Your mother?' said Dancey incredulously, as if mothers should never look like that. 'This is your *mother*?'

'Yes.' Ruth smiled again and Dancey blurted, loud and sudden as a child, 'Where is she?'

'She died when I was a baby. I never saw her, not to remember, anyway.' Ruth thought of the presence she used to sense out at the crossroads in Barinjii when she was a girl, and how, even now, on the borders of sleep, she sometimes had that sweet feeling of being rocked and held.

'I wish I'd never seen *my* mum!' exclaimed Dancey with a sudden fierce passion, and again Ruth said nothing, and the girl's words seemed to float in the air and give out their meaning over and over again.

'How did she die?' Dancey asked at last. 'Your mum? Did she kill herself?'

The question might have seemed surprising until you remembered that Dancey's mother had done just that. More or less.

'She died in a car accident,' answered Ruth.

'Was she drunk? Was she wasted?'

Ruth took a deep breath. Sometimes it was hard. 'Of course she wasn't,' she said, struggling to keep any edge of anger from her voice. 'She was only a young girl with a baby.'

'A young girl with a baby,' echoed Dancey thoughtfully, and though she said no more, her rainy grey eyes held an old expression which said quite plainly, You can be a young girl with a baby and still be wasted. Carefully, expelling a tiny breath from her lips into the air, she put the photograph back in its place beside the one of Margaret May and studied the empty space beside them. 'Didn't you have a dad?' she asked.

Dad, thought Ruth, and saw him standing at the crossing gates, leaning on his old bicycle, waving at the train that was carrying her away. Poor Dad.

'Didn't you?' persisted Dancey.

'Yes, I did.'

'How come there's no photo of him, then?'

'We just weren't a photo-taking family, I suppose.'

'Did you have a husband?' asked Dancey. 'Kids?'

'No kids,' said Ruth. 'I had a husband once, when I was younger. For a little while.'

'Didn't take, eh?' The girl smiled knowingly. Sometimes it was difficult to believe she was only thirteen.

'No, it didn't take,' agreed Ruth.

'Better off, I'd say,' said Dancey, and then added in the same low passionate voice she'd used about her mother, 'It's better to have no one. Then you can't get—' she broke off. The blind knocked on the windowsill again – tappety-tap, tappety-tap – and the girl spun round, white-faced, as if that innocent sound had been someone come for her, knocking at the door.

'Dancey,' Ruth began, but the girl broke in, 'I'm going outside, out into the yard for a bit.' She turned and almost ran from the room.

'Don't go too far away,' Ruth called after her. She swung her legs over the edge of the bed and at once felt a sickly warmth strike up from the polished boards beneath her feet. The heat got everywhere. 'I'm going to get us some breakfast in a minute.'

There was no answer, only the sound of footsteps running down the hall. The front door squealed open and a wind with the smell of smoke upon it rushed into the house. Far away there was the faint splutter of a motorbike and somewhere high above the roof, a sudden wild screech of cockatoos.

Two

Dancey ran blindly across the prickly grass of the front yard, anger fizzing inside her head, sparking and spitting like fireworks in the dark. Her heart banged so hard against her ribs it could have been the fist of some crazy little person hidden in there, struggling to get out. She threw her arms out and began to whirl in circles, round and round and round, then stopped and stood for a moment with her head tossed back, waiting for the dizziness to subside. 'Stupid, stupid, stupid!' she muttered furiously, while the sun banged down on the top of her head like a big hot punishing hand. 'Will you *never* learn?' She pinched the soft flesh on the inside of her arm, hearing her own treacherous voice back there in the bed-room, saying, 'It's better to have no one. Then you can't get—' She'd stopped herself there, at least. She hadn't said the rest of it, which was 'messed up and then left all on your own.' But she'd *almost* said it, hadn't she? And then Ruth would have known that there'd been a time when Dancey had wanted people to love her. She'd gone and told her about the garden, too, the garden with the beautiful trees and the shining lake that had come into her mind back when she'd been a little kid at Roseland. At least she hadn't told her about the peacock and the dark-haired man; she'd kept them to herself.

Telling private stuff was something Dancey had crossed off, crossed right out of her life; it was something you should never, never do. You told them stuff and then when it turned out later that they didn't want you, you'd gone and given little bits of yourself away. For nothing! They forgot, of course; most of them couldn't wait to put Dancey Trelawny right out of their tiny minds, but it still left you feeling stupid, and ashamed. Soft.

She *was* getting soft, because look at what she'd gone and done when they were walking home from the community meeting last night! Ruth had been worrying about the fires, *really* worrying, so you could feel it coming off her, like vibrations in the air. Even in the dark you could see tears shining in her eyes.

Dancey herself loved fires: the snap and hiss of them, the roar and rush, the mad smell of smoke in the air like there'd been from the fires over at Mount Hay. Under control now, the firemen had told them at the meeting – but there'd be more. It hadn't rained once, not properly, all through the spring and early summer, and now the *real* summer was here – January – and still it hadn't rained. The wind raged, and the bush had a dry powdery look about it, and a knowing, waiting air. Dancey ran to the fence and climbed up onto the bottom rail, staring out towards the horizon where there was a long smudge of grey – you couldn't tell if it was cloud or smoke or simply brimstone sky. Dancey didn't care! Let it burn!

Ruth was dead scared, though. 'I can't bear to think about it, Dancey,' she'd said last night as they'd trudged towards home down Hayfield Lane, which was no more than a bumpy track hemmed in by trees and dry scrub on both sides. Some of the trees had black scorched trunks so you could see a fire had been through before. Five years back, Ruth had told her. 'I wasn't living here then,' she'd said, and that's when she'd started going on about how she couldn't bear to think about fire: 'all the old people who won't be able to get away in time, and all the animals, Dancey! Running, trying to escape, and the birds, falling from the sky—' she'd broken off with a little choking sound and that's when Dancey had done it, broken all her rules, actually reached out and clasped Ruth's hand. Only for a second, because she realised at once what she'd done and quickly snatched her hand away. But to do that! To actually reach out and *touch*. Touching was a thing Dancey had crossed out for good. You never touched them.

'Come and give us a birthday kiss, love,' Janine, the last foster mother, had coaxed her, pouting her lips and making kissie sounds. Dancey wouldn't, she wasn't going near her.

'Ah, c'mon, don't be like that! It's my birthday!' Janine had cried, but even when Barry, the foster dad, had given Dancey a backhander for being a spoilsport and upsetting people, she'd stood her ground. She wasn't kissing any of them.

They'd taken her back, then, like they all took her back, as if she was a toy they'd bought that didn't work properly. They'd told on her; Janine had told that snatch-faced social worker, Sandy Jimpson, that Dancey had no proper feelings: 'No emotions, like. She's a little psychopath!' Then Barry had put his oar in. 'Like those serial killers,' he'd said, 'those ones you see on the TV.'

Dancey jumped down from the fence and though it was boiling hot she began to run around the lawn in circles again, because thinking about stuff that had happened, about Barry and Janine and Sandy Jimpson and all the others, *everything*, made her body want to *move*, and move fast, as if in the running she could somehow get rid of the bad things, leave it all behind. Round and round she went, until she was so dizzy she couldn't stand up anymore but fell down on the grass and lay there looking up at the sky. The grey smudge on the horizon was bigger now, but she still couldn't tell if it was smoke or cloud or just the colour of the sky. The wind whistled in the telephone wires, hoo-eee! hoo-eee! and there was a sudden loud snap! as a branch broke from a tree and tumbled to the ground. She jumped up and went over to the gate, but she couldn't see where the branch had fallen; there were so many trees out there, all crowded together, soughing and swaying in the wind.

From far down the lane came a faint putt-putting sound and then the postman rounded the bend on his yellow motor-scooter and came bumping down the track. Mikey, he was called, a fat, squidgy boy with hair the colour of old axle grease and a great big pimple blazing crimson in the middle of his forehead like a fiery third eye.

'He's Melissa Lygon's big brother,' Megan Stoyles had informed her, but Dancey was none the wiser, she didn't know who Melissa Lygon was, she'd only been at the school for two months and the kids all seemed alike to her – a lot of squealing white rats locked up in a pen. The only ones whose names she remembered were the kids in her home class and the girls in Megan Stoyles' gang.

''Nother hot one, eh?' Mikey greeted her as he stopped his scooter by the gate and rummaged in his bag.

What a brain! Dancey tossed her wild black hair. 'Yeah.'

'Fires are out over at Mount Hay.'

'There'll be more,' said Dancey. 'Lots more.'

'Ya reckon?'

Dancey nodded. 'Everything will burn,' she said. 'The houses and the people who can't get away. And all the animals will be running, the kangaroos and wallabies, the foxes and the rabbits and the sheep left in the paddocks, running and running – and the birds will fall out of the sky.'

He goggled at her. 'Ya reckon?' he said again, and handed her two letters, one big and one small and both addressed to *Ruth Gower, Hayfield Lane, Medlar, NSW.*

'Saw you at Macca's last Saturday,' Mikey said. 'Over at Woodie.'

'Yeah?'

'You were with Megan Stoyles and that lot.'

'None of your business where I was,' said Dancey. 'Or who I was with.'

The snub didn't stop him. 'You ever fancy going out some-where a bit more classy with yours truly—'

Dancey cut him short. 'There's nowhere I'd fancy going with yours truly in a billion years,' she said and his pudgy face turned scarlet and his whole body flinched away from from hers. His eyes had a look of terror in them, as if he thought she might suddenly fly though the air and sink her teeth into his throat.

'If that's the way you want it, then,' he mumbled.

'It most certainly is,' said Dancey, deepening her voice, making it sound so cold and severe you'd have thought she was Matron Trapcott back at Roseland. Mikey shot her a frightened glance, stamped the pedal on his scooter and lurched away down Hayfield Lane.

Dancey slid the two letters down the neck of her tee-shirt and made her way round the side of the house, where a row of tall fir trees formed a shady green tunnel against the wall. It was a place she liked a lot, a place where she could be private and think about her garden, imagining the big trees and the paths which shone white in the moonlight and the tiny little waves which lapped at the shore of the lake, *shusha, shusha*. She *knew* that garden, not because she'd been there, but because it was somehow *her place,* it was in her blood. Once she'd fallen asleep out here beneath the fir trees and the dark-haired man and the peacock had come round the side of the house, she could sense them, watching her sleeping. The dark-haired man was whistling his song very, very softly, as if he thought she might be worn out from all the bad things that had happened and he didn't want to wake her up.

Dancey settled down comfortably on the deep carpet of pine needles and took the letters from her shirt. The smaller one in the white envelope was from Mrs Fiona Howe, 21 Hopeton Street, Barinjii, NSW. Mrs Fiona Howe was Ruth's best friend; they'd grown up together in this little town way out in the country and to Dancey it seemed an utterly amazing thing that they'd kept on knowing about each other for so long. She couldn't imagine that ever happening to her, couldn't imagine anyone would ever bother with her for years and years or that she'd ever bother with anyone. People moved on, or they died, and after a while you just forgot. Even her mother's face was growing dim. She could remember the sound of her mum's voice all right, because sometimes it woke her up in the middle of the night, that steady whine she used to get when she started up saying all that stuff about the way she hated the sight of people and how she'd be better off dead.

Only little Frankie's face stayed clear and lovely in Dancey's mind.

She put Mrs Fiona Howe's letter down on the pine needles and weighted it down with a small round stone. She turned her attention to the other, larger one which was more of a packet than a letter, a big brown envelope fastened with tape and covered with lines of postage stamps which said, India India, India.

She knew what was inside. In the evenings when Ruth was out watering the garden, Dancey went into the study and examined the emails on the computer and the letters in the desk drawers. Ruth might not have any kids of her own, but she had godchildren, lots of them; the shelf along the wall was filled with their photographs, and the lopsided vases and pottery dogs and cats they'd made when they were little kids, and the photographs of their wives and children now they were grown up and even getting old.

What are godchildren? Dancey hadn't actually asked this question, but Ruth must have read it on her face because she'd answered. 'Godchildren are your friends' children. It means I go to their christening – that's when they get their names in church – and promise they'll be good.'

'And are they?' Dancey couldn't help asking.

'Oh yes,' Ruth had said, smiling. 'But not because of me.'

Ruth had friends all over the place: teachers like she'd been, old students, people who read the books she'd written, people who wrote books themselves. The one who lived in India, the one who'd sent this letter, was called Bansi and he was Ruth's favourite of all. This would be the special photograph of his family and their new baby he'd been promising to send.

The tape was already half unstuck; Dancey pulled it off and slid the photograph out into the light.

She looked down at Bansi's family. They were standing in a garden, a beautiful garden which was a bit like hers, with green lawns and gravel paths and waves of little white flowers flowing over a stone wall. There were big trees and a pond with a statue standing in the middle, even a peacock, his tail spread out like a jewelled fan. It wasn't *her* peacock, of course, only one that looked like it. The man who'd been Ruth's student was quite old, at least forty, and the woman beside him wasn't all that much younger. They weren't particularly beautiful or handsome but their faces had a kind of light shining from them, which Dancey thought might be happiness.

At Roseland little Frankie's face used to have that light on it when he saw Dancey coming into the room.

The man wore a grey suit, and the woman a silk sari in the brilliant colours of the peacock's tail, and the baby was wrapped in the kind of shawl that Ruth wore on those rare evenings when the heat dropped and a cool change swept in – a deep crimson shawl with gold embroidery, so light and fine that you could pass it through a ring.

Dancey hadn't believed the thing about the ring. 'Show me!' she'd demanded. 'Show me how it goes through!' So then Ruth had taken off the old wedding ring she wore on her right hand, which wasn't her own ring, but had been her mum's, twisted a corner of the shawl, and then, like a kind of magic, the whole thing had slid right through, floating in the air like smoke from a genie's lamp.

Can I do it? Dancey had wanted to ask, but she didn't, because it would have made her sound like a kid, and then Ruth had said, 'Here, you have a go,' and the great silky cloud had floated through the little ring for Dancey, too.

'Bansi gave me that shawl when he got his PhD,' Ruth had told her, and then Dancey had wanted to ask what a PhD was, but she held the question back; she hated letting on that there were things she didn't know. She kept the question in her mind and looked it up later in the library at school; it was always better to do stuff on your own.

As well as the new baby lying nestled in its mother's arms, there was a little girl in the photograph, a little girl in a pink dress resting her head against her father's side. She looked about four, which had been Frankie's age – though the little girl was a proper four year old, with arms and legs that worked and a mum and dad and a new baby sister or brother and that whole beautiful garden to play in every day. There'd be a house somewhere, too, a big beautiful house to go with everything else.

Dancey had been four when she and Mum had lived with Mick in the caravan park up at Maclean. She'd liked it there; she'd liked the way you could hear the sea at night, like a sweet breathy voice that went, 'La la la.' It hadn't lasted though. Mick hadn't lasted and the place hadn't lasted and soon they were back in a squat somewhere in Sydney and Mum was on something and it wasn't long till Dancey was in care.

She held the edges of the photograph and gazed right in. Sometimes she had the feeling with pictures of places she liked that if she stared into them hard enough, really concentrated, then the picture might open magically and she could slip right in. She thought that this might have been what little Frankie had been doing at Roseland when he gazed through the window at the sunlight shining on the leaves: wishing himself out there, away, part of the sun and the breeze and the dancing light. Perhaps that was where he'd gone.

It had never happened to Dancey though, and it didn't happen this time; she stayed where she was, in the cool private place beneath the fir trees, round the side of Ruth's house in Hayfield Lane, Medlar NSW. And that was probably a good thing, because imagine if she *had* got into that photograph! Imagine: a great wind would rush through the beautiful garden, the big trees would rattle and bend and sway, the peacock would run away screaming and the little family would rush into their house and Dancey would be left on her own, standing there until someone inside made a phone call and the police came to take her away.

But it wasn't the beautiful garden that she longed for, even though it was so like hers. It wasn't the garden which brought the sudden raw pain to her heart and a gnawing in her stomach like she hadn't eaten in a long, long time. It wasn't the flowers or the peacock or the baby's shawl or the little girl's pink dress.

It was love.

Love was in that photograph.

'I love ya,' Rolly Miles had said to her in Roseland. Rolly was nineteen and worked in the kitchens, Dancey was ten and Mum was drying out somewhere. She hadn't liked Rolly all that much but she'd let him mess her about. When the Roseland people found out they said it was abuse but Dancey knew it wasn't. She'd let him, hadn't she? Even though it had hurt. And she'd let him because he'd said that word to her. Love. Back then, if anyone said that word to her, Dancey was gone. Even to see it written down, in one of Mum's magazines, or scrawled up on a wall, would make her eyes jump and the gnawing feeling come.

She knew now that the way Rolly Miles had used the word, and the way the kids in the street family had used it, didn't mean anything you could rely on. It wasn't love, that. But knowing this hadn't stopped the word from getting to her, calling up the idea of the real true thing, the thing that made her raw to be without, and which she had a pretty good idea she'd never ever have. Her fingers trembled at the edges of the photograph. The love that was shining out of it was the real true thing. You could see it in the way the mother was holding the baby, in the way she looked down at it and the baby looked back at her; you could see it in the way the father was resting his hand on the little girl's head, gently, lightly, but you knew it meant he'd look after her for ever and ever, amen.

'Dancey! Dancey!'

Ruth was calling. 'Dancey! Breakfast's ready!'

Dancey slid the photograph back into its envelope and thrust it down the front of the big green tee-shirt which Ruth had bought for her, all new, at David Jones. 'Would you like one with something written on it?' Ruth had asked. 'Or a picture?' but Dancey had said no, she wanted it plain, because the green colour was so beautiful it reminded her of the song the dark man whistled, walking with the peacock in the garden that was Dancey's special place. 'Coming!' she called, scrambling to her feet and hurrying round to the front verandah. 'I'm coming!' She forgot about the other letter. It lay on the pine needles beneath its little stone, and a gust of wind lifted one corner and then passed on and let it lie.

Three

Oh it was hot, so hot. Ruth pulled up the blind in the kitchen and stared out into the glare of the front yard.

Everything was achingly dry: the grass scorched brown, the leaves on the plum trees limp and curled, a veil of powdery dust hanging over the earth. The sky was a hard, ungiving blue and far off on its rim was a long smudge of grey. Smoke?

The fires at Mount Hay were out; she'd turned on the radio to check the Fire Bulletin, and then the RFS website, to see if any new ones had started overnight. There'd been nothing so far, but it was early, only half past seven, the morning had just begun. Temperatures would be in the high thirties in the mountains today and strong winds were predicted, strong winds that had been blowing since midnight. It was another day of Total Fire Ban, the sixth since Christmas, three weeks ago. There'd been no mention of rain on the forecast; so the grey smudge on the horizon was probably smoke drifting in from the extinguished fires. After all this time, rain was unimaginable.

Dancey was out there, whirling in circles round the lawn. She stopped suddenly, and the way she stood there, head thrown back, hands on hips, while the wind tugged at her skirt and the tangles of her blue-black hair, reminded Ruth of Helen Hogan beside the creek at Barinjii, standing in exactly that way, hands on hips and head tilted, scowling at Ruth and telling her, 'Just remember that you know nothing, okay?' It had been true, thought Ruth, though Helen Hogan probably hadn't known all that much more than she did.

Dancey did look a little like Helen; she had the Barinjii girl's pale translucent skin and the blue-black hair. And Tam Finn's rainy grey eyes. An idea stirred again in Ruth's mind; an idea which had been growing on her ever since Dancey had come, and which she'd struggled to keep at bay because it was so fantastic, so like wishful thinking, wanting something to be true. It couldn't be true, except – the dates were right, and Dancey's grandmother had been called Helen: Ruth had seen the name on Dancey's record in Sandy Jimpson's office, a record so brief it made your heart ache for the child. *Mother: Tammy Trelawny; Father: Unknown.* Tammy Trelawny's mother was Helen Trelawny, and Tammy's father was also recorded as unknown. A list of girls' names, Ruth had thought, no fathers around – and then unexpectedly she remembered the little wooden statue in the church at Barinjii, of which her nan had been so fond.

Could Helen Hogan have married a man called Trelawny in Sydney all those years ago? And given his name to the daughter she'd got from Tam Finn? Tammy Trelawny? So that Dancey, with her blue-black hair, pale skin and rainy grey eyes, could be the grandchild of Helen Hogan and Tam Finn? 'Tam Finn's child,' Ruth said aloud, watching the girl climb up on the front fence and stand staring out into the bushland.

Be sensible, she told herself – Dancey was simply one of the many thousands of children whose family had vanished and left her on her own.

'That's your emergency bag,' Ruth had told her a few days back, pointing to the blue backpack she'd prepared and placed ready in the hall.

'Emergency bag? What for?'

'In case a fire comes and we have to leave. I've put in a torch and a water bottle and a change of clothes, and I've left room for anything special you might want to take with you.'

Dancey had stared at the bag, her face quite blank, her body tense as strung wire. But the tension hadn't been about the fires. 'Are you coming too?' she'd asked, her eyes fixed on Ruth's face.

'Of course I'm coming! What did you think? That I'd go off on my own and leave you?'

Dancey hadn't answered that. 'Where's *your* bag, then?' she'd asked suspiciously.

'It's in my room; I haven't finished packing yet. Then it'll be out here, right next to yours.'

'Ah,' the girl had sighed, and her small heart-shaped face, the whole of her slight body, had relaxed and Ruth had realised that for Dancey Trelawny there were far worse things than fires – and being left was one.

'Would your brain boil, inside your head?' she'd asked on the way home from the community meeting last night.

'What?'

'If a fire came, when it got you, well – you know how your

brain sort of floats in watery stuff? So would the watery stuff start boiling, inside your head? And your brain get cooked? Like a big dumpling in a pot of soup?'

'I don't know,' Ruth had replied, revolted. 'Anyway, if it did, you wouldn't feel it.'

'Wouldn't *feel* it? Wouldn't feel your brain boiling?'

'No.'

'*Why* wouldn't you feel it? This kid I knew in America pulled a pot of boiling water off the stove when no one was looking, and boy, did she *feel* it!'

'People in fires generally die of smoke inhalation before the flames get to them,' said Ruth, struggling to sound calm.

'Does it hurt? Does smoke inhalation hurt?'

Yes, thought Ruth, imagining the terrible searing of the throat and lungs, the struggle for air where there was no air, the agonising suffocation. 'No,' she'd lied.

'S'pose it's not a bad way to go,' Dancey had observed in the strange little elderly voice she used sometimes, and they'd walked on in silence until she said, 'I've met lots of people whose brains boil, and they're nowhere near a fire.'

Ruth held her breath, but the girl had said no more. She was thirteen and she knew all kinds of horrors. 'My mum tried to put her head in the gas oven once,' she'd remarked last Sunday lunchtime as Ruth was sliding out the chicken in its roasting tray. 'Only it wouldn't fit, see? Her head? She couldn't get it in properly. You know why?'

'No.' The tray had rattled as Ruth set it on the kitchen bench. Her hands had been shaking.

'She'd forgotten to take the shelves out!' whooped Dancey.

'And when she caught on that they were actually *there*, and that's why she couldn't get her head in the oven, she wanted me to take them out for her – she was too pissed to hold things properly. But I wouldn't do it, so then she got up and clouted me and I ran off and she came after me and she forgot all about doing herself in. For that time, anyway.' She'd stared at Ruth defiantly and Ruth hadn't known what to say. She was never sure if Dancey's sudden dreadful confidences were meant to be confidences or attempts to shock her. The stories, whose truth she never doubted for a moment, could even be some desperate form of letting go – she noticed how the girl's eyes would widen as she related such episodes, how she'd talk faster and faster, almost to the point of breathlessness. And she realised that no matter how offhand and unfeeling the girl might appear, Dancey was afraid of the deep chanciness of the world in which she'd grown.

'My family,' she'd confided another time, 'my street family, that is, the one in Portland: they bashed up this old tramp down in the underpass, bashed him with sticks and chains and bars and stuff and then, guess what? We all ran off and left him there.'

Ruth hadn't been able to stop herself from asking, 'Did *you* bash him?' She'd expected an outburst but instead Dancey had greeted the question with a kind of sober thoughtfulness. They'd been washing the dinner dishes and she'd put the cup she'd been wiping carefully on the bench and stood there quietly in the lighted kitchen, tea towel in her hand, while she sorted out her memories and her feelings, trying to get them right. 'I couldn't,' she'd said at last. 'My hands weren't free.'

'Your hands weren't free? Oh, Dancey, you mean someone had tied you up?'

'No, no, not like that. *I* was holding them behind my back, tight as anything, so I – so I couldn't do anything.'

'Ah!' Ruth had almost gasped her relief.

Now she began to lay the table for breakfast: the two yellow bowls and plates, the glasses, knives and spoons, the cereal, the bread for toast, the Vegemite and honey and strawberry jam.

'It would be all *ash*,' Dancey had said last night in Hayfield Lane.

'What would be all ash?'

'All this—' she'd waved both arms in a grand gesture that encompassed the lane with its canopy of great overhanging trees and beyond it, the whole night landscape of valley and mountain bathed in smoky moonlight – 'all *ash*. Like the end of the world. Whoosh! Everything gone.'

'Oh Dancey, don't!' Ruth whispered, because hadn't she imagined this herself? Especially on the wild windy nights of this fire season, when helicopters rattled overhead and there was a sound of sirens on the highway. 'Don't!' The word had come out in a kind of sob.

And then Dancey had slipped her hand into Ruth's. Only for the merest fraction of a second, sliding it out again so quickly that Ruth had wondered whether she'd imagined those warm fingers inside her own.

'Don't expect affection,' the social worker had warned her. 'They don't do affection. There's a time when children learn how to love, learn the words, the actions, and Dancey's missed it, I'm afraid.'

'But surely,' Ruth had protested. 'Surely, if she's given love—'

Sandy Jimpson had shaken her small head slowly, definitely, from side to side. 'They just don't know *how*, Ruth. They're damaged. They don't know what love is.'

But in Hayfield Lane last night, there'd been that fleeting touch of Dancey's warm fingers, which had comforted Ruth all the way home.

She opened the fridge to take out the jug of orange juice; breakfast was ready now. Glancing through the window she saw that Dancey had gone from the front yard. She was surprised by the cold drop of her stomach, and then the lift of gladness when she called the girl's name and heard the sound of big feet running round the side and Dancey's untroubled voice calling, 'Coming, I'm coming!' as if she was an ordinary undamaged child.

four

There was a red mark and the beginning of a bruise on the girl's arm. 'You've hurt yourself,' observed Ruth from across the table.

'Bumped into a tree,' said Dancey. 'You know, mucking round, doing whizzies like some stupid little kid, not looking where I was going.'

'Ah.'

There was a silence in which Dancey took a slice of toast from the rack and stared at it hard.

Ruth fiddled with a spoon. After a moment she said gently, 'Where did you get your name, Dancey?'

Dancey dropped her toast onto the plate. She glared at Ruth across the table. 'Mum gave it to me,' she hissed. 'And I hate it, I told you. *Helen*: hate it, hate it, hate it! It's pissweak, just like *her*. She said it was *her* mum's name, but if she had a mum, I never saw her.'

'You didn't?'

'Nah, something happened to her before I was born.'

Something happened to her. She'd have been the same age

as me, Ruth thought, thinking of Helen Hogan. She remembered Helen in her red dress down by the creek and thought, yes, it was easy to imagine something happening to her. 'She came to grief,' sighed Ruth, and Dancey stared at her and echoed, 'Came to grief,' making the phrase sound as if grief was a special country into which Helen Hogan might have wandered. The idea that Helen was this child's grandmother was most likely a complete fantasy; all the same Ruth decided that next time she went into town she'd check if there was a death recorded for her. And she'd check if Helen Hogan had become Helen Trelawny, and if she'd had a daughter called Tammy, father unknown.

'Anyway,' said Dancey, 'I don't reckon I had a gran.'

'How do you mean?'

'I reckon my mum just grew out of the ground, like a toad-stool or something,' began Dancey, and then stopped short, as if she'd only just remembered how her mum was dead and buried, back down beneath the ground. She rubbed at the red mark on her arm, rubbed and rubbed at it.

'Your real name's what I meant,' said Ruth gently. 'Dancey.' She remembered Tam Finn telling her about his peacock, that first time in Starlight Lane. 'His name's Dancer,' he'd said. She leaned towards the girl. 'Where did "Dancey" come from?'

More than half a century ago at Barinjii Infants, Ruth had a teacher called Mrs Lupin. When Mrs Lupin wanted silence in the classroom, she'd pinch her thumb and forefinger together and draw a wavy line in the air, in and out and in and out, as if she was sewing a seam. 'Let's *sew* our lips together,' she'd tell the class. '*Sew* our lips up tight.' And she'd demonstrate with her own lips, drawing them into a mean, straight line.

Dancey did this now, setting her lips together so tightly it seemed no words could ever force their way through. She picked up a knife and began to spread butter on her toast, so ferociously that the bread shattered into pieces on her plate. 'It's *my* name,' she said at last.

'Yes, I know.'

Dancey attacked the toast again.

'Here, leave that.' Ruth whisked the plate of crumbs away and handed Dancey a fresh one, with a new piece of toast. 'I just wondered where you got it from, that's all. It's an unusual sort of name. There's a character in a book—'

'It's *mine*,' said Dancey again. 'Not from any old book.' She stared at Ruth with narrowed eyes. 'Why do you want to know?'

'Well, it suits you so,' said Ruth, smiling. And she meant it: the name suited the girl's heart-shaped face and blue-black hair, the flying moods, and the thin taut body which was so swift and light. 'It's like – your essence,' she said.

'What's essence?' said Dancey, forgetting herself for a moment and asking another person straight out the thing she needed to know.

'The heart of Dancey,' Ruth replied. 'Exactly *you*.'

It was the way Ruth had spoken the word 'you'. It must have been, Dancey thought afterwards, the way her voice sort of lingered on it with a kind of tenderness, as if 'you' meant someone who was special to her. Important, even. Whatever the reason, or even if there was no reason, only a sudden fierce longing she couldn't control – without for one second meaning to do it, Dancey told.

It was a precious secret, as precious as the garden and the peacock and the dark-haired man, and she'd never shared it with a single soul, and now she went and told.

'One time when Mum was really out of it,' she began, 'when I was ten, before we went to America, they put me in this place called Roseland.'

'They put me in this place called Roseland.' The matter-of-fact way the girl spoke these words sent a little wave of cold right down Ruth's spine; Dancey might have been describing a toy grown sick of, put away in a box.

'And there was this little kid in there,' Dancey went on, 'in the hospital part. He was called Frankie and he was only four.'

'Four,' echoed Ruth.

'Yeah – but if you hadn't known he was four, if you hadn't read it on the chart at the end of his cot, you might have thought he was a baby. He had this big head, but the rest of him was really small and spindly, and he couldn't do anything,' – Dancey shook her head suddenly, very fast, as if she was trying to shake something awful away – 'he couldn't sit up, or stand by himself, or walk, or talk, only lie in his cot and turn his head a bit to stare out the window. And he made these sounds, sort of like words, but not quite, you know?'

Ruth nodded.

'So there was a big tree outside the window,' Dancey went on, 'and it had a little mirror tied to one of its branches, one of those little mirrors they have for birds, and on bright days it would catch the sun, see? And then all these little ripples of light would come through the window and run across the ceiling over Frankie's cot, and they'd move like they were dancing and Frankie would watch them and move his mouth a bit and you could see he was trying to smile. It wasn't a proper smile, like other people's, but he meant it to be.' Dancey leaned her elbows on the table, cupped her chin in one hand, and gazed earnestly at Ruth. 'They said he couldn't talk, that he'd never be able to, but you know what? One day when we were watching those reflections dancing on the ceiling, he suddenly smiled at me and sort of slid his eyes to the reflections and he said, "Dancey, dancey!" He meant the reflections were dancing. Honest he did!'

She leaned forward, grey eyes fixed eagerly on Ruth's face. 'He did, didn't he?'

'Of course he did.'

'And that's where I got my name,' said Dancey. 'From Frankie. Frankie gave it to me.'

Ruth swallowed. Beneath her pity and sorrow for the little boy's story there was a small pang of disappointment. She'd been hoping Dancey might say she'd got her name from a story her mother had told her: about how when her gran, Helen, was young she'd been in love with this boy in the country who had a peacock called Dancer . . .

'So did you tell them about Frankie?' she asked. 'The people at Roseland? Did you tell them how he'd said a real word? That he knew the reflections were dancing? That he could understand things?'

'Wouldn't have done any good if I had,' said Dancey in that same dull matter-of-fact voice. 'They never believed you in that place. And it was too late, anyway.'

'Too late? How do you mean?'

'Well, next day Frankie was gone, see.'

'Gone?'

Dancey didn't seem to hear. Her face was faraway with grief.

'You mean, he died?' said Ruth softly, and Dancey came back and said, 'Dunno. He might have. You never knew, when kids like him were gone: whether they'd died or just been taken away to some other place. No one ever said, and if you asked they just told you it was none of your business.'

'You must have been sad, though.'

Dancey shrugged her narrow shoulders. 'No use blubbering,' she said. 'Things happen, that's all.'

But she had been sad. Back at Roseland she'd been a baby. Not in years perhaps, because she was already ten, but inside, where it mattered, she'd still been soft and weak like a very little kid. She hadn't worked out yet that it didn't pay to care, that the only thing caring did was to get you all upset, and sometimes into trouble, too. She'd bawled for days when Frankie had gone. 'Dancey, Dancey, Dancey,' she'd repeated to herself, standing beside the empty cot, watching the sun patterns dancing on the ceiling.

It occurred to her now, though she didn't tell Ruth, that the feeling she'd had for Frankie might actually have been love: that little catch of the heart she'd felt walking into his room and seeing his face turn towards her – that was love, surely. That was proper love, that was the real true thing. And Frankie had loved *her* – there'd been that look on his face when he'd seen her at the door, that shining tender expression like the people had in Bansi's photograph. His lightsome look, she'd called it, because it was as if his whole tiny body, every single bone and cell and pore of it, had suddenly filled up with light.

When she lost Frankie – that was the first time the peacock had come, and the dark-haired man beside him, singing his beautiful song, which she'd known was meant for her. She'd seen the garden before, seen it often on the edge of sleep and knew it was real, and that it was *her* place, but she'd never seen the peacock before, spreading his tail to show her his colours, the jewelled greens and purples and blues, never heard the dark-haired man whistling the pure true notes of his song. They'd come to comfort her because Frankie was gone.

Suddenly, right there at Ruth's kitchen table, without the slightest warning, tears sprang into Dancey's eyes. She fought them back; she hadn't cried since Roseland, she couldn't start crying now, when she was big, when she was thirteen, not in front of another person. She jumped to her feet, scraping the chair back over the wooden floor.

Ruth stretched out her hand. 'Dancey!' she said. 'Dancey dear!'

Dancey flew into a rage. 'Don't call me *dear*!'

Ruth's hand went to her mouth. 'I'm sorry, I—'

'Leave me alone!'

Dancey rushed past her, but halfway across the room she stopped dead and Ruth watched as the girl drew herself to-gether: she saw the brave tilt of Dancey's head and the way she held her narrow shoulders, straight and defiant, as if she was saying with her body, the only thing she had, 'I don't care!' Just as Tam Finn had done that last time in Starlight Lane, walking away from her out into the night. Exactly like him.

As the girl walked out of the kitchen and disappeared into the hall, Ruth was almost certain that Dancey Trelawny was Tam Finn's child.

five

'We're goin' into town,' Megan Stoyles' voice boomed from the telephone. 'Ya wanna come?'

'Into the city?' asked Dancey.

There was a pause, then Big Meg spoke again. 'Nah. Just into Woodie.'

Woodie was Woodfall, the largest town in the mountains, two train-stops or a bus ride away.

'You comin' or aren't ya?'

'I guess,' said Dancey. It was halfway through the morning and there was nothing much else to do. And she wanted to keep clear of Ruth; Ruth had seen her almost cry.

'Meet ya down the bus stop in half an hour then, right?'

When Dancey reached the shelter by the highway, only three of the gang had shown. It was a small gang anyway: there was Megan, the big fat blonde, her sidekick Folly Walker, a tall, watchful girl with dusty dreadlocks that no one but Big Meg would be dumb enough to trust. Then there were the white rats, as Dancey thought of them, Kimberly Brent and Janis Taylor, two scrawny girls with whitish hair which fell about their tiny faces and pale blue, pink-rimmed eyes.

And Laura Laurence, who was the sort of girl from a good home you sometimes found in real street families, trying to be wild. All of them, even Big Meg, were impressed that Dancey had been in America and lived as a street kid there. Except for Laura Laurence, they were even impressed that she'd been in care. This exotic history was the reason Big Meg had let her in the gang. Not that Dancey had really wanted to be in it – but sometimes you got a bit bored, and then you tagged along.

The white rats had stayed home. 'Said it was too hot, the losers,' growled Big Meg as the dusty old bus came lumbering into view.

'Too hot!' marvelled Folly, rattling her dreads.

They scrambled up the steps and settled right down the back. 'Yeah, too hot, that's what they said,' repeated Big Meg, rolling her flat blue eyes. 'Both of 'em. A bit of hot weather and they want to lie down and die! Ya gotta be tougher than that! I mean, it's a long summer, right?'

'Right,' agreed Folly. 'It's a long summer.'

Laura Laurence didn't say anything. She turned her head and stared sadly through the back window at their little town growing smaller in the distance, as if she was some poor displaced person driven from her home. Dancey had the feeling that, not today perhaps, but pretty soon, Laura Laurence was going to cross the gang right off.

'Yeah, you gotta be tough in this old world,' rumbled Big Meg, stealing a sideways glance at Dancey.

None of them were tough, reflected Dancey, not even Big Meg. They weren't even really wild. In term-time they wagged a bit of school and did a bit of stealing from the shops at

Woodfall, all red in the face, panic-eyed and gasping as they sidled out the door with their pathetic loot: tubes of cheap makeup, flimsy little scarves, hair stuff and the kind of jewellery you'd find at the bottom of a supermarket Christmas stocking. In a bigger place they'd have been nabbed right away – as it was the girl behind the checkout at Sam's Treasure Trove had laughed at them – no loss to her if a bit of junk went missing.

One day last month the gang had ventured into the city, and Dancey had tagged along. Janis and Kimberly had gone to school. In town they hadn't been able to think what to do. The wind was blowing coldly off the harbour and no one had wanted to go across to Manly. They wandered round the shops for a bit and finally decided on a movie, sitting in a row and eating popcorn and ice-creams like little kids on a birthday treat. The cinema had been full of soppy old couples holding hands and even older ladies who had bigger gangs than theirs and kept popping out to the toilets and then coming back and asking each other what was happening on the screen.

Afterwards, Dancey couldn't remember what the movie had been about. All the way through it she'd been thinking of the street family she'd belonged to back in Portland. Normally, she tried not to think of that time, but she'd been sitting next to Laura and the smell of her apple-scented shampoo had suddenly brought it all tumbling back. Not that the street family had used apple-scented shampoo – no, it was a kind of memory of opposites: the scent of Laura's shampoo, so clean and sweet and somehow innocent made her remember the lice and the sores the street kids had. And how, after a bit, no matter how hard you tried, all your clothes and your hair and even your skin got this coffin smell, like you'd been buried under the earth and someone had dug you up. In the soft reflected light of the big screen, Dancey had looked along their little row of clean shiny girls and thought how there wouldn't be a single mark on their bodies, not one bite or sore or wound. She'd slipped a hand beneath her tee-shirt and felt round the back for the little scarred hollows where Drago's belt buckle had bitten in that first time she'd tried to run away.

In the street family you had marks and you made marks, too, if someone betrayed the family or didn't show respect. Traitors had to be punished, and you had to take your turn at punishing like everybody else, because that was the family's way. And you had to do it, or the family would do it to you. They would, they'd done it to Star when she'd refused to take her turn. They'd beaten her, then taken all her stuff and kicked her out, dazed and half naked, to wander in the street.

Dancey could remember the feeling of beating someone, punishing: how it felt as if it wasn't really you that was doing it, but some other person, while the real you was crouched down, small as a peanut or a sesame seed, small, small, small, deep inside you, eyes closed and hands over its ears. Even to remember that time made her feel sick. She'd closed her eyes and sensed the beautiful garden begin to open round her, the paths and flowers, the big heavy-leafed trees, and far off the sweet glimmer of water that was the lake.

In the gloom of that big city cinema, Dancey had begun to cross off the bad things from the past. 'I'll never hit anyone again,' she'd said aloud, and then Big Meg had leaned across Laura's slight body and hissed, 'You goin' mad or what?'

and at the sound of her voice the beautiful garden had faded, disappeared.

TODAY, when the bus dropped them off at Woodfall there was nothing going on. The sun was blazing, and half the shops were closed because of the heat. The main street had a deserted look; tourists were staying down in the city. They trudged up the hill to Sam's Treasure Trove, but having to work in the heat had got to the girl behind the checkout counter and she was in a mood. 'You kids come in here and I'll call the cops!' she roared. 'And your poncy school as well!'

'Stupid cow!' cursed Big Meg as they scurried out into the street. 'She's got it in for me because she fancies Tice and he won't even look at her.'

'Why should he look at her when he's busy lookin' at you?' smirked Folly.

'You got it,' Big Meg agreed.

Tice Brady was Big Meg's boyfriend, or so she said, a blubbery boy whose roly-poly limbs reminded Dancey of the rubber turrets of a kid's bouncy castle.

'Wanna go up to the hot bread shop?' suggested Folly, nudging Big Meg's arm. 'You might see him there.'

'Nah, he's not workin' today.'

'Tired him out last night, didya?'

The big girl leered. 'Whaddya think?'

What Dancey thought was that they were virgins. All the gang would be virgins, every one of them, including Big Megan Stoyles. 'Saving themselves for Mr Right,' she thought with a smile – Matron Trapcott had told her that, way back in Roseland, after the trouble with Rolly Miles.

A huge sign stood outside the post office. *Total Fire Ban*, it read, and the big scarlet letters seemed to pulse out into the air. They stared at it in silence until Folly said in a low voice, 'My dad says this whole place is going to go up any day.'

'Pissweak,' growled Big Meg.

Dancey thought of Ruth and how scared she was of fires. But Ruth wasn't pissweak; Dancey had a feeling that if a fire ever did come roaring down Hayfield Lane, Ruth would be brave.

'He got the car serviced last week,' Folly went on, 'so we could leave the moment we heard there was a fire in the mountains that might come here.'

'If everyone leaves the road'll be blocked,' said Laura. 'Nobody'll be able to move. People would get burnt up in their cars.'

A gust of wind set the flags on the roof of the post office rippling: whomp whomp whomp, they went, whompey-whomp – and the girls looked up, because it was such a spooky sound.

'They tell you to hose down your house when the fire's coming,' said Folly. 'But my dad says if a fire's coming there won't be any pressure because the firemen'll be using all the water. Nothing'll come out of your hose.'

'And what about the people who don't have cars?' whispered Laura. 'They stop the trains when there's a fire. How will those people get away?'

'And what if a fire starts at night and comes really fast, when everyone's asleep?' said Folly, and her face lost all its cunning and went soft with fright. 'You'd wake up and it would be too late.'

'Will youse shut up!' roared Big Meg. 'I'm sick to bloody death of hearing about fires!'

The way she stood there, legs apart, huge trainers flat to the ground, arms folded across her enormous chest, you could just tell how she'd be at forty, thought Dancey. A big old mum standing on the doorstep yelling at her kids, 'Get in here, youse lot, before I get the strap! Tea's on the table!'

'*Sick* of fires!' the big girl said again, and now there was something like a sob in her thick voice.

Everyone went quiet.

Folly patted her friend's arm.

'It's so *hot* here,' Big Meg whimpered.

'Let's go back in the bus,' suggested Folly. 'Look, see – it's just comin' back round the corner there.'

'And what'll we do *then*?'

'We can go to Laura's place,' said Folly with a sly glance at the other girl. 'She's got that nice big air-conditioned basement. Haven't you, Laura? With a rumpus room and all.'

'Yes,' said Laura in a little voice. She stood on one foot and scratched her calf with the toe of her sandal, and Dancey thought she looked uneasy, even worried, but all the same she nodded and said to the others, 'Okay, we can go to my place if you like, sure.'

six

Laura's house was the last one on Cloudy Ridge; at the end of her garden the land fell away to a deep blue valley from which the further mountains rose like steep grey walls. The four girls stood huddled together on the last little strip of dry brown grass, hair whipping round their faces, staring down into the trees.

'There's a path,' said Laura, pointing to a rough pebbly track down the side of the hill.

'Where's it go?' asked Folly.

Laura shrugged. 'Nowhere really. Just down into the bush. There's a view.'

'The bush,' sneered Big Meg. 'I hate the floggin' bush. And views. I hate views too.'

The wind roared, snapping at her words; the treetops threshed and fumed.

'Whew! Imagine tossing a match in *there*!' gasped Folly.

Dancey sucked in her breath. As if Folly would be game. As if any of them would be, even Big Meg Stoyles. They had too much to lose – their big fancy houses would burn up, and all their glitzy clothes: the tiny skirts and spangled tops, the soft leather shoes and the expensive runners in icing sugar colours; their makeup and perfumes and big squashy bags, their trashy jewellery and their best jewellery: the gold chains their dads had given, the strings of pearls from nans. Their mums and dads would burn and even they might burn. Dancey imagined Big Meg's legs lying dead on the black earth, the fat in them sizzling, bone showing through, a puff of singed blonde hair blowing in the wind. A phrase stirred in her mind, from some school, someone reading in a room – *a rag, a bone, a hank of hair* – that's all Big Meg would be. The phrase made her think of little Frankie lying in his cot, and then the next day not being there and she had this feeling that what you loved might always disappear. You were better off without it.

The wind roared again, slapping at their faces, tugging at their hair.

'C'mon!' yelled Big Meg. 'Let's get inside!' and they ran in a bunch round the side of the house to the basement door. Laura pushed it open.

'Oooh, it's dark! I'm not goin' in there!' cried Folly.

'Didn't know you were scared of the dark, Fols,' grinned Big Meg and Folly blushed and said, 'I'm not. It's just—' and then Laura switched on a light, revealing a long room with a flight of narrow stairs at one end, a big table in the centre, an old couch and several battered armchairs pushed up against the wall. 'Hurry,' she urged them, 'before the heat gets in!'

They surged inside and Laura shut the door. Big Meg flung herself down on the sofa and gasped out, 'That's more like it!'

for the air was deliciously cool in here – except for a certain stuffiness, and a faint eerie whistling of the wind behind the walls, you'd never guess at the kind of day outside. You could be anywhere; you could be away down in the city where you didn't have to worry about the weather except for what outfit to wear, where fires were no more than chatter on the radio and no one had ever heard of emergency bags.

Dancey sat down on one of the armchairs and looked around. The house was built into the side of the hill; at the far end of the basement the ceiling came down lower and the tiled floor gave way to hard packed earth. It was like a cave. Suitcases were piled up in there, and boxes, and a roll of old carpet, and the spaces between were full of shadows, damp and dark. There was a musty familiar smell.

'Anything to drink?' Big Meg demanded. 'Any Fanta? Coke?'

'Sorry,' said Laura, 'we've only got lemonade.' In the shelter of her own house, her voice sounded firmer, more sure.

'Lemonade it'll have to be then,' sighed the big girl, wrinkling her little pug nose.

'Folly?' asked Laura. 'You want some lemonade?'

'Yeah, I'm gaspin'.'

'Dancey?'

Dancey didn't answer, she was still staring towards the cave at the end of the basement.

'Dancey?' Laura said again.

'What?'

'You want some lemonade?'

'Oh – yeah.' She added, 'Please,' and Laura smiled.

'Right. Back in a minute then.' Laura ran lightly up the stairs.

Dancey huddled in her chair. She held her arms round her body as if she was cold. Her legs trembled. The cave, the darkened earth, reminded her of that place beneath the overpass where the street family had their home. She remembered the dog shit and the dark stains on the ground which could have been oil, or blood, or anything, and how she and the other girls had swept stuff clear and laid sheets of old cardboard they'd collected from the backs of factories and shops. And how the cold still struck through the cardboard and the sleeping-bags and through their very bones – and a hardness like iron, and the coffin stink in your clothes.

Never! Dancey promised herself in the depths of the old armchair. 'I'm never gonna be in a place like that again!'

'Talking to yourself again?' sneered Big Meg.

Dancey shook her head.

Upstairs a door closed softly and a moment later Laura appeared on the steps with a tray of glasses and a big jug of lemonade.

'Crisps?' wondered Big Meg, when drinks had been poured, but Laura said gamely, 'We're not allowed.'

'Not *allowed*?' Folly raised her pencilled brows. 'You're not *allowed* to have crisps?'

Laura flushed. 'Mum says they're too salty. We've got some nuts and raisins if you like.'

'Forget it,' said Big Meg, and took a huge swig of lemonade. Then she burped so loudly the sound filled the room.

Folly burped too, even louder, and Big Meg shrieked, 'Good one, Fols!'

'We'll have to be a bit quiet because Mum's home,' said Laura.

'Thought your mum worked down the library.'

'She does. But she's home today because Frankie's sick.'

Frankie. Dancey went still; it seemed utterly strange to hear someone else say that beloved name. Dancey said it every single night before she went to sleep – she'd done that ever since the morning she'd gone into the room at Roseland and Frankie hadn't been there.

'Frankie? Who's that?' Big Meg asked Laura.

'My little brother.'

'What's he got?'

'Mumps.'

'Mumps! Geez! Lucky we're not boys, eh?'

Dancey had a funny faraway feeling inside her head, it was almost as if she wasn't really sitting in the armchair, but floating up near the ceiling, looking down at them all. Distantly, she heard Big Meg's loud voice going on about mumps and the damage it could do to a boy's equipment. 'Shrivels everything right up!'

'Frankie's only four!' Laura replied indignantly.

Like her Frankie, thought Dancey. Her Frankie had been four.

Then she was back in the chair and Laura was bending towards her.

'Are you okay, Dancey?' she was saying.

'Yes, yes, I'm okay,' said Dancey quickly, sitting up straight and pushing back her hair. 'Just – can you tell me where the bathroom is?'

'She means the dunny,' sneered Big Meg. 'Only she's too polite to say.'

'It's upstairs, next to the bathroom. I'll show you,' said Laura. Dancey picked up her shoulder bag because somehow she knew she wouldn't be coming back to this room, and then Laura took her hand and together they went up the stairs.

'You're so pale!' Laura exclaimed when they reached the top. 'Would you like me to get Mum?'

'No, no, I'll be all right,' said Dancey. 'It's – it's just the heat. It makes me feel dizzy.'

Laura nodded. 'I know. I fainted once in school assembly. It was awful; two of the teachers had to carry me to the sick-room, and everyone was staring.' She smiled at Dancey again and unexpectedly Dancey found herself smiling right back and though there was no sign of the garden or the peacock she thought she heard the dark-haired man saying, 'She'll be a good friend for you, Dancey.'

Laura pointed down the hall. 'The bathroom's there,' she said. 'That blue door, see?' She peered at Dancey in a worried way. 'You sure you'll be all right?'

Dancey nodded and then Laura said, 'Well, okay then. Call if you need anything. I'd better get back to the others.' When she said 'others' Laura rolled her eyes at Dancey to show she wasn't included in those others, and then she hurried away down the stairs.

Dancey stood by herself in the cool green hall and thought about Frankie. Of course she knew Laura's Frankie couldn't be *her* Frankie: there couldn't be some kind of miracle where her Frankie hadn't died but only been sent to another hospital and then miraculously adopted by Laura's family. Things like that just didn't happen in the world. And even if they did happen, once in the very bluest of moons, it wasn't possible anyway because Laura's Frankie was four *now* and Dancey's Frankie had been four way back at Roseland, three whole years ago. If he'd lived, Dancey's Frankie would be seven.

Frankie hadn't been sent anywhere. He'd died. She'd known that very morning when he wasn't in his cot, and there'd been a nurse in the room folding up his clothes.

'Where's Frankie gone?' she'd asked.

The nurse hadn't answered but Dancey had known from the look on her face.

She tiptoed down the Laurences' hallway, past two closed doors, one with a china plaque which said, *Laura Sleeps Here*. The third door was open a little way, and a woman's voice drifted out, saying something about having to make a start on the dinner, and then a child's one asking, 'And *then* will you come back?'

Dancey peeped round the edge of the door.

She saw a little boy sitting up in his bed, in a way that Frankie never could sit up. His face was flushed and his eyes had dark shadows beneath them, but he was a perfect and beautiful child.

'Have a rest now,' his mother was saying, and the little boy lay back against the pillows, and she touched his eyelids lightly with her fingertip, one by one.

'You're my best boy,' she told him. 'You're my own dear

darling,' and she dropped a kiss on the top of his small rough head and out in the hall Dancey felt that sudden raw pain in her chest, and the gnawing hunger for something that could never ever be hers. She turned and hurried away along the hall, down the steps, past the door to the basement, through a long living room and out into the blazing day, where the hot wind rushed at her and the grey smudge on the horizon had sent long thick fingers out across the sky. She fled down to the end of the garden and onto the rough track that descended steeply into the valley, and as she ran, slipping on pebbles, grasping at the thorny branches of bushes, the little boy and his mother flickered like an old film inside her head: over and over the mother's fingertips touched her son's eyelids, her lips kissed his hair. 'You're my best boy,' she said. 'You're my own dear darling.'

For a long time Dancey had told herself that love was only people fooling themselves; it was stuff that wasn't real, that lasted no longer than a blob of fairy floss on your tongue before it melted away. Except she kept on *seeing* it, the real true thing: people saying goodbye at railway stations, looking into each other's eyes, mothers standing at school gates, little kids flying out to them, dads in the park pushing swings. She kept on seeing it and she couldn't stand to see because it made the gnawing hunger well right up inside and even the garden and the peacock and the dark-haired man singing his song for her couldn't seem to make it go away.

'I don't care! ' cried Dancey as she stumbled down the hillside. 'I don't care!'

There was no one to hear her. The track ended in a small

lonely clearing between the tossing trees. The dry grass prickled at the back of her legs as she sat down and the earth itself was hot as the skin of a feverish child. Below the clearing the land fell away sharply, the trees, their thin trunks slanted, went on and on like soldiers marching down to the valley floor. The hot wind blew and the treetops surged like breakers in a big wild stormy sea.

Dancey reached into her shoulder bag for the photograph of Bansi and his family. She held it in her hands and deeply gazed. See! There it was: love was real, it was just that people like Dancey and little Frankie never got it: no one wanted them, not really, and if they said they did, it was only for a little while. Ruth would get sick of her soon – she thought of the way she'd slipped her hand into Ruth's last night: how pathetic could you get? It was stupid to think a person like Ruth, who had all those friends and students and godchildren, would need any comfort from *her*. Dancey Trelawny was totally all on her own. It isn't fair! she thought, and heard a dim chorus of carers' voices replying, 'Life isn't fair, Dancey.'

Big Meg had a mum and dad who loved her, even though she hated them – and so did Folly and Kimberly and Janis. She closed her mind on Laura's mum, the sweet voice saying, 'my own dear darling,' the light kiss laid on the top of a small rough head. A kind of rage flared up inside her; why was she the only one who had to be all on her own? She raised a hand to her mouth and gnawed on her thumbnail – she'd like to take everyone away from everyone so they'd all have to be alone like her! She stared down at the photograph; she gripped the edges with both hands and tore. She tore it carefully, in tiny little strips, taking the people away from each other, so that everyone was separate; so the woman had no arm around her, and the little girl had no father's waist to lean her head against, and the baby was all on its own. There!

She reached for her shoulder bag and took out the box of matches. As she struck the first one she could almost sense the dry trees watching her, as if they held their breath. First she burned the mother and father, and then the baby and the little girl; she turned the little family into ashes, and blew them right away.

'I don't need *anyone*,' she whispered, but she knew it wasn't true. She took a second match and struck it, while in front of her the dry bush waited and the trees went still. The match went out. She waited then; she waited for the garden to come and the peacock to spread his jewelled feathers and the dark-haired man to sing his song. They didn't come, though Dancey could feel them somewhere quite near, still like the trees, as if they were waiting for her to know what she had to do, as if they were saying silently, 'You're a big girl now.' She lit another match and tossed it down into a clump of dry grass. After a moment, a tiny flame shot up and leaped into a litter of dead leaves and they began to smoulder, and from somewhere she thought she heard a small sad sigh. The wind blew, coaxing the smouldering leaves into a line of little flames, and as she watched the flames grew taller, they ran along the edge of a small dead branch and licked at the bottom of a banksia.

A fire was beginning.

The way the wind was blowing, a fire would go back up

the hill to Laura's house and then down through the reserve to Hayfield Lane.

There was a new feeling inside her now – it reminded her of the time the street family had found the old tramp sleeping in their place beneath the overpass and got stuck into him with their boots. Dancey had stepped back into the thick shadows of the concrete pillars so the others wouldn't notice that she wasn't joining in. She'd clasped her hands behind her back so tightly that the nails had driven in, and stood there watching the family's faces: she'd seen how at first it was as if they didn't want to do it, but then they couldn't stop themselves; they *had* to. How timid they'd looked at the first kick, but then there was a second kick, and then more and more and more, and you could see their faces changing, lit with an emotion it was impossible to name. It was like they *had* to. It was how she felt now about the fire: she didn't really want to, but something inside her *had* to have its way. She took another match.

The fire would get her, too, but that didn't matter, it never had mattered what happened to her; there was no one to feel sad. The banksia bush was beginning to burn quickly now, its lower branches whistling and singing with a little, racing flame. Its curling leaves smelled heavenly; Dancey drew in a long breath – the raw hungry feeling had gone; now there was only a great flatness like a landscape of poisoned ground. The peacock and the dark-haired man had left her on her own; for a moment she thought she heard the distant sound of the man singing, but it was only the voice of the fire. The fire sang and crackled; something popped and flew right through the air.

Everything would turn to ash.

'I can't bear to think about it, Dancey,' she heard Ruth's voice saying. 'All the old people who won't be able to get away in time, and the animals . . . running, trying to escape, and the birds, falling from the sky—'

'I fell out of the sky when I was little,' whispered Dancey, 'and no one even saw.'

'The heart of Dancey,' Ruth said softly, 'Exactly *you*,' and her voice held that same tenderness Dancey had heard in Laura's mother's voice as she sat with her little boy, the tenderness that shone from the faces of the Indian student's family, or sounded in the dark-haired man's song – the tenderness that was the real true thing.

Dancey sprang to her feet and rushed towards the fire. She kicked at the banksia bush. She kicked and kicked, she stamped, she scooped up handfuls of sandy soil and threw it over the burning twigs and leaves. 'Out! Out! Out!' she cried. 'I'm crossing you out, see! You're gone!'

And little by little the fire *was* gone, flaring and glaring, sulking and smoking and dying, till it was no more than an occasional red glint among the ashes, which Dancey covered with stones and armfuls of the hard dry soil. She put the fire out. She buried it. Then she waited; she stood there for half an hour to make sure it couldn't begin again. The wind dropped. A new little breeze came, whispering and cool. The trees sighed with pleasure. The sky was all grey now, and a big drop of water fell suddenly on the top of her head. Other drops fell in the dust. They fell on the warm earth above the ashes, and the warm earth hissed and went black and wet and held no danger anymore.

The garden floated round Dancey, its lawns and paths and big kind trees. She turned and the peacock was there, spreading its glorious tail, and the dark-haired man came and looked into her eyes and said gently, 'Go home now, little one.'

'Home?' asked Dancey, and he smiled the most beautiful smile she'd ever seen and said, 'Go home to Ruthie.'

The rain was falling. She ran up the hill and turned in the direction of Hayfield Lane. The air was cold and the trees dripped; it was as if the whole world was changing. A flock of white cockatoos flew over, so soundless they might have been cut out of cloth.

seven

There was a new fire over in the Hartshorn Valley; Ruth heard the news on the radio. The Hartshorn Valley was thirty kilo-metres to the west, but thirty kilometres was nothing on a day like today. She went to check that the gutters were still free of rubbish; when she opened the door, the heat came at her like a blow. It had a thickness about it now, clammy and solid against her skin, and when she looked up she saw that the sky was grey, a soft foamy grey the colour of cobwebs. The wind had dropped. 'Please rain,' she whispered as she hurried down the side path. 'Oh please, please rain.'

She had no real hope, all spring and summer there'd been such afternoons: the sky would cloud and the wind die down and it would seem that at any moment the rain would begin to fall. But the dry minutes stretched into hours and then in the evening the wind would rise again and the cloud thin into wisps and the moon and stars shine through, and at the end of the ten o'clock news the jovial announcer, safe down in the city, would say happily, 'Tomorrow's going to be another hot one.'

The leaves of the young peach tree she'd planted hopefully

last year hung like sad little rags from the branches; all the greenness had been sucked out of them, they'd lost their light, like her dad had done after the accident in which her mother died. In the old people's home he'd had a special chair beside the big window in the dayroom where he'd sit from breakfast till bedtime gazing out into the garden. 'He seems quite happy in himself,' the matron used to say when Ruth came to visit. 'Never a cross word.'

He'd died two years ago.

The gutters at the back of the house were clear; Ruth walked round to the shady side beneath the firs. Here too the gutters were still free of debris, but as she turned to go inside again her glance fell on something small and white lying beneath one of the trees. A piece of paper? An old envelope blown there by the wind?

It was a letter, still sealed. A small pebble sat in the centre of the envelope, weighting it down. Ruth picked them up. For a moment she studied the pebble, then dropped it onto the ground. The letter was addressed to her and was from Fee, postmarked Barinjii, two days ago.

So it would have arrived in the post this morning. How had it got round here? Sometimes the postman left letters hanging from the box and they fell out onto the ground. That might have happened. And today, the wind could have swept it across the grass, even tweaked it round the corner of the house, till it fetched up here beneath the firs. That *could* have happened.

Only there was the pebble. The pebble couldn't have got there by itself. Someone had placed it on the envelope, to weight it down against the wind. And then that person had forgotten, because she'd heard her name being called. She pictured Dancey out in the front yard this morning, remembered the distant putter of a motor-scooter from further down the lane, remembered how, when she'd called her to breakfast, Dancey's running footsteps had come from round the side.

She could have dropped it. Dancey could have collected the post, intending to bring it inside, and then come here – it was one of her favourite places – and the letter had drifted from her pocket and she hadn't noticed it fall. Ruth shook her head impatiently: why was she fooling herself like this? Dancey had taken the letter. Ruth had known for a long time that when she was out of the house, Dancey spied. She had found little traces: a slight rearrangement of the contents of her drawers, the laptop shifted slightly closer to the edge of the desk, nearer the chair, so that someone small could operate it comfortably.

Nothing had ever been taken, and Ruth had let the matter go. Dancey was only checking, she told herself; the spying in Ruth's things was simply part of the girl's effort to feel a little bit secure. Dancey wanted to know about Ruth so that she could begin to feel she might be safe. Ruth thought of Dancey's warm hand in hers last night and the way she'd drawn it back, quickly, as if she'd been terrified. 'They don't *do* affection,' she heard Sandy Jimpson's thin voice saying. 'They can't.'

'They're afraid to,' said Ruth.

She went back into the house and sat down at the kitchen table to read Fee's letter.

'They've drained Skelly's dam,' wrote Fee. 'They're going to build houses there. Remember how I used to say that if they ever did that, there'd be bones at the bottom of the dam, the bones of Tam Finn's girls?

Well, I was right and I was wrong, Ruth. There were bones down there all right, a whole skeleton of bones. But it wasn't one of Tam Finn's girls – it wasn't Kathy Ryan or Ellen Lester or even Helen Hogan: they all went to Sydney after all, eh? Sydney's a big place; girls can vanish down there as well as at the bottom of Skelly's dam. (Though I'm glad you never did.)

It was him, Ruth. Tam Finn.

Old Mrs Finn identified the bones. Sergeant Mercer went out to Fortuna and brought her back to the hospital where they'd taken what was left of poor Tam Finn. Old Mrs Finn, I called her, but ancient would be a better word. She's ninety-seven, people say. I mean, think of it, Ruth: she's not Tam Finn's mum, she's his gran! And he was the same age we were, just about; so, work it out: old Mrs Finn must have had his dad when she was about fourteen! You should see her, Ruth! I did – not stickybeaking, honest, just happened to be passing the hospital on my way to get the milk – she's very tiny now, very tiny and thin, like some kind of bird, but she'd not hunched over like so many people that age, she stands straight and she walks straight and she looks people straight in the eye. And what eyes she has, Ruth! Sharp and bright as needles; you get the feeling that if she looked at you hard, it would hurt. Poor Tam Finn.

Anyway, she identified him. There was a watch with his

name on the back, and some shreds of a blue shirt, and that old ring he always wore, remember? The snake with red eyes that was swallowing its tail? I always thought that ring was sort of scary. I know you liked him when we were girls, but I thought Tam Finn was scary, too.

All the same, he was a human being. And no one cares what happened to him, Ruth. No one knows if he fell in the dam, or if he jumped, or if someone pushed him, and no one wants to know. The Finns thought he was living some-where down in Sydney – he went down there not long after you left – and when they never heard from him again they simply thought he couldn't be bothered with them. And they couldn't be bothered with him; they'd written him off long ago.

Now I know he was weird, but honestly, Ruth, imagine just forgetting about someone like that, someone who's your own son, your own grandson! What's wrong with people? Sergeant Mercer told Mattie that old Mrs Finn looked at the watch, and the ring, and the shreds of blue shirt and then down at the bones and all she said was, 'Yes, that's my grandson. That's Tam Finn. He was always headed for the bottom of something.'

There's not going to be a memorial service or anything like that. But I suppose, when you think about it, who is there to remember? None of us knew him, not really, not even Tam Finn's girls. I don't know if there's going to be any kind of enquiry or if anything would come from it – Sergeant Mercer says it was all a long time ago.

A long time ago!

But that's our time he's talking about, Ruthie! The time when we'd just left school and I was getting married and you were off to university – and it makes me feel funny when Sergeant Mercer thinks our time is ancient history. Despite the kids and grandkids, to me it seems like last summer, and sometimes, when I'm walking across the paddocks or down along the creek, I'll play this game: I'll close my eyes and concentrate, and almost believe, Ruthie, that when I open them I'll be back in that time again. I'll be seventeen, and Mum and Dad and Gran will still be alive, and any moment when I look up, I'll see you running along the track towards me – in that blue skirt you used to wear, remember? The blue skirt with the pockets? How lovely you were!

And still are, of course.

Come visit soon, and bring your Dancey – we're longing to meet her.

All love and kisses, xxx
Fee

So Tam Finn was gone. All these years Ruth had had a sense of him, far away yet always in this world, travelling in exotic places: in India and Africa, the high plateaus of Ladakh, the romantic cities along the old Silk Road. She'd had this day-dream that when he was old and she was old, too, they'd come back to Barinjii, and she'd be walking down Main Street and see him across the road and she'd go up to him and say at last, 'Look, here I am.'

He'd never got to be old. 'Not long after you left,' Fee had written, so he'd still been a boy. She read the letter through again, and found herself crying. It was the blue shirt that did it: she could remember the way it had hung from his narrow shoulders, and how the breeze had blown the cloth against his body, revealing his thinness, the shape of his bones.

'Let me,' he'd pleaded the last time she'd seen him. 'Let me, oh, let me!' and she'd wondered later if he'd been saying, 'Help me.'

Perhaps he had been – for that unhappy boy, roaming the paddocks of a small country town, it would have been the same; sex would have helped him, but only for a little while. 'Oh Tam,' she whispered. His shadow had been at the back of her whole life: every man she'd gone out with, every lover, even the man she'd married for a while, had seemed some-how wrong after Tam Finn; as if she was still looking for him, like she'd been looking on the train that took her away from Barinjii, staring through the dusty window of her compartment as the country darkened, hoping for a glimpse of him.

She imagined him strolling down Starlight Lane in his blue shirt, up the hill and across the paddock towards Skelly's dam. He'd be whistling one of his old hymns: *Come down, O love divine, Seek now this heart of mine*— Going into the water he'd still be whistling; he'd go down and then he'd come up again, and down and up again and each time he'd be whistling until the very last time when the water closed his mouth for good. And then there'd be silence and darkness, and a few last bubbles floating on the surface of the water, with the last notes of the hymn trapped inside, and the great stars looking down.

'He was a boy,' she said angrily, aloud. 'Only a boy.'

A sudden loud pattering made her glance towards the

ceiling. For a moment, she didn't take it in: birds quarrelling up there on the roof? A possum fallen from its nest in an overhanging tree? Then she realised it was the sound of rain-drops and her heart lifted, even though she knew they'd stop in a moment, like they always did, and the wind would grow stronger and the cloud would thin into long tattered veils and the sun would come out again.

But the pattering went on, it became louder, soon it was a roar. Ruth sprang up from the chair and ran down the hall to the verandah: the grey sky was so low it seemed to touch the treetops; the rain fell in torrents, in sheets, in streams. Already there were shining puddles on the dry lawn. A glorious scent of water and the peppery perfume of soaked earth and grass and leaves drifted from the bush.

The rain is raining all around, she heard Tam Finn's young voice reciting, *It falls on fields and trees, it rains on the umbrellas here, And on the ships at sea.* 'Dancey!' she called. 'Dancey! It's raining! Come and see!'

There was no reply. Of course – Dancey had gone into Woodfall. She'd get soaked. Soaked.

Behind the roaring of the rain there was a deep quiet, and from this quiet, faintly and far off, she heard her name being called.

'Ruth! Ruth!'

Somewhere out in the lane.

She ran down the verandah steps and out to the gate. The grass squelched wonderfully beneath her feet, Hayfield Lane was running with water, out in the bush she could hear the rushing of the waterfall and above it the voice still calling her name – and there down the lane she saw a small figure running towards her, and it seemed to Ruth that everything in her life had led up to this moment: the accident at the crossroads, Barinjii, Tam Finn, the years between, the letter inside on the kitchen table – everything had led to this, the thin dark-haired girl, clothes streaming, running up the lane, calling out her name. 'Ruth!'

Ruth held out her arms and Dancey ran into them, sobbing.

'I tore up your photo!' she gasped. 'I tore up your photo, Ruth! The one the Indian man sent of his new baby and his family! Bansi! I tore it into tiny little bits and then I burned it up! I'm sorry!'

'It doesn't matter,' said Ruth, pushing the dripping hair from the girl's cold forehead. It was wet and sticky with dust but it had such a wonderful, living feel.

'It does matter! It was beautiful!' sobbed Dancey. 'There was a baby and a little girl—'

'He'll send us another one,' said Ruth.

Us. Dancey's grey eyes seemed to leap at the word. They glowed.

'Will he?' she asked, her voice trembling. 'Will he? Send – *us* – another one?'

'Of course.'

They stared at each other. How like him she was: that pale heart-shaped face, the blue-black hair, the rainy grey eyes – every gesture, every expression was that of Tam Finn's child.

But it didn't matter if she wasn't, thought Ruth. All around them, a new kind of balance was forming in their world – the heat and dust and danger was giving way to rain: the tanks

246

would fill, the grass grow green, people would sleep sound at night. Tam Finn had been lost, but Dancey Trelawny was found – that was the real true thing. She put her arm round the girl's narrow shoulders and turned towards the house. 'Come on,' she said. 'Let's go inside.'

acknowledgements

HYMNS AND SONGS

Tam Finn's hymns are: 'Cradling Children in His Arm' –
Nikolai F G Grundtvig, 1783-1872; tr. Johannes H V Knudsen,
and 'Come Down, O Love Divine' – Bianco de Siena,
d. 1434, tr. Richard Frederick Little
Father Joseph sings: 'Glory be to God in Heaven' –
Michael Perry, Catholic Worship Book, 1985
Nan sings: 'Nut-Brown Maiden', a Traditional Scottish song
Tam Finn recites: 'Rain', from *A Child's Garden of Verses*,
by Robert Louis Stevenson, 1913
Barinjii Anglican Church sings: 'All Things Bright
and Beautiful', by Cecil Alexander, 1848